BIOPECULIAR

GIGI GANGULY
BIO
STORIES OF AN
PECU
UNCERTAIN WORLD
LIAR

Published by Westland Books, a division of Nasadiya Technologies Private Limited, in 2024

No. 269/2B, First Floor, 'Irai Arul', Vimalraj Street, Nethaji Nagar, Alapakkam Main Road, Maduravoyal, Chennai 600095

Westland and the Westland logo are the trademarks of Nasadiya Technologies Private Limited, or its affiliates.

Copyright © Srijani Ganguly, 2024

Srijani Ganguly, writing as Gigi Ganguly, asserts the moral right to be identified as the author of this work.

ISBN: 9789360450977

10 9 8 7 6 5 4 3 2 1

This is a work of fiction. Names, characters, organisations, places, events and incidents are either products of the author's imagination or used fictitiously.

All rights reserved

Typeset by SÜRYA, New Delhi

Printed at Parksons Graphics Pvt. Ltd

No part of this book may be reproduced, or stored in a retrieval system, or transmitted in any form or by any means, electronic, mechanical, photocopying, recording, or otherwise, without express written permission of the publisher.

For Coco, Snoopy, Lizzie, Neffi, Cleo, Zulu, Oli, Orla and Bren, and all the dogs and cats who have been a part of my life.

Contents

Head in the Clouds	1
Call for Kelp	8
Toothache	16
A Year (Not Quite) Alone in an Alien Wilderness	26
Sort Sol	34
Ceaselessly Sea Follows	41
Hunter	43
Cocoon	47
Losing	61
Polarspeak	67
Corvid Inspector	71
Crown Shyness	112
Moss	116
The Forest of Plenty	124
Whirlwind	127
A Storm of Stings	132
Solastalgic	139
The Golden Bird	151
Barking Up the Wrong Tree	162
Hats and Other Coverings	169
Nemesis	175
Eatflicks	180
Acknowledgements	187

Head in the Clouds

The old man lifts his head and counts the clouds hovering above him, high up in the sky. Twenty-five. One less than yesterday.

'Hmm,' he says out loud.

He's just stepped out of his house, pausing only for the count, and now he moves again, walking on a cool November morning towards his daughter's house. She lives next door, but there is a large expanse of farmland—hers—he must walk past first. He takes the narrow, muddy path on the outer ring of the crops, carefully and slowly placing his feet on the ground.

At one point, a coughing bout takes hold of him and he stops, clutching his sides, eyes watering in pain. Above, the twenty-five clouds shimmer and shiver—one of them even turns grey momentarily.

'I'm fine,' he tells them once the moment has passed.

There are so many photos in his daughter's house. Pictures of him and his wife on their wedding day, of their daughter as a baby, as a teen, a grown-up, and then there are photos of her children too—two girls, two years apart in age. Both off to college now.

Always, in pictures taken outside, there are clouds hovering above them.

'What are you looking at, Dad?' his daughter asks, two mugs of tea in her hands.

'Just ... thank you,' he says, taking an offered mug. 'Just looking at the photos. There are so many of them.'

She looks at him, concerned. 'Dad,' she says, 'you do remember that you gave us this house? That this is our family house? You wanted to live in a small cabin, in an open field—'

'Yes, yes,' the old man says. 'I just never realised there were ... so many photos, so many memories in here.'

He grabs hold of her free hand and brings her closer to a picture above the fireplace. 'Look at you here,' he points at her five-year-old self, grinning, with half of the milk teeth gone. 'You were so small then.' He pauses and looks at the one next to it, a photo of him and his wife, and his then fourteen-year-old daughter. He feels a sudden, overwhelming pressure inside his body. His eyes tear up. 'Your mother would have been so proud of you, of the strong, accomplished lady you are today.'

'*Dad.*' His daughter trembles.

Outside, the clouds grumble and softly thunder. It begins to drizzle.

'What's wrong?' she asks him, sniffling.

'Nothing.'

'And the clouds?'

'Oh, they're just sad. One of them went missing last night. The smallest cumulus. But don't worry, I'm going to look for it.'

'Dad, I don't think—' his daughter starts, but he puts his right hand up like a stop sign and says, 'It's alright, I'll be safe. They'll be with me.' He turns his gaze upwards.

She looks unconvinced. Knowing there's not much she can say when her father has made up his mind, she still tries. 'How will you even find the cumulus? Where will you go? Are you really, *truly* sure about this?'

The old man smiles. 'I have an inkling of where it could be. I know how they feel. I just ... know them.'

His daughter frowns as she realises how he's planning to travel. 'You're not going to use the clouds, are you? At your age?'

'I'll be fine,' he says.

'But what about ... I read this in a newspaper ... Aren't there reports of cloud-seeding companies kidnapping clouds for their work? How can you be sure that the cumulus hasn't been *taken*?'

'It's the nature of clouds to wander, and sometimes they wander too far.'

'But, Dad, you can't be sure where it would've gone ...'

'I'm a cloud-herder,' he says, with finality. 'I can see the signs in the skies.'

Truth be told, the old cloud-herder *was* uneasy about the cases of cloud kidnappings and disappearances. Some of his friends had already lost a few cumulus and cumulonimbus in the past couple of months. He didn't want the same to happen to his herd as well. He'd already racked up a lot of guilt over the years. He couldn't believe how he had constricted them, keeping them in low-pressure nets when he'd started training them. It was necessary at that point, he knew. He had to keep them together so they wouldn't stray. It also allowed the clouds to bond with him, and now they always hovered above his head. But now he knew what he did not know then: clouds, like birds, were not meant to be caged.

Back when he started the job, cloud-herding was as simple as any other sort of farming. You took the clouds out to places that needed a spell of rain, and let them graze the required time. It wasn't a hundred per cent accurate, everything depended on the mood of the clouds: if they had any strength in them, if they wanted to rain for a long period of time. But when technology barged into their lives, it all changed.

First came the electric lassos. Then it was the turn of moisture machines. And now, everywhere he looked a cloud-seeding company had sprung up in the open country, in between farmlands and mills. They fed clouds all sorts of things to induce rain, treating them most cruelly, without any semblance of care.

A cloud was a gentle being. It did humans a great service, providing them with showers, drizzles and pourings. But it also needed to rest, to stay idle and wander the skies.

The cloud-herder carefully folds the letter in half, then folds it once again. He writes his daughter's name on it and places it neatly on his dining table. Next, he puts on a woollen hat, covering his ears, and a heavy jacket for the cold winds he'll encounter on his journey. In his pockets there are nourishment bars. At the door, he slips his feet into fur-lined boots. Finally, he's ready.

He steps out and whistles twice. A medium-sized cumulus drifts down to his side, floating effortlessly as it comes to a standstill in front of him. The old man finds the grooves in the fluffy, airy cloud and climbs on board. A terrible, shaking cough strikes him at that moment and he struggles to breathe through it. Tired and defeated at the end of it, he clasps the cumulus tightly and asks it to take him upwards, towards the waiting herd.

When he looks down, he can see the tiny figure of his daughter running from her house to his. She suddenly stops, noticing him airborne, and waves her hands above her head, perhaps asking him to stop. But he can't hear her from that far.

His daughter knows him very well, she has always figured out his inexplicable actions before anyone else. This time, it has taken her a while.

The old man has always found the air at the cloud level to be pure and freeing. It's always colder than the ground conditions, but it's soothing and peaceful. That is all he wants now.

He lets the clouds lead. They cross over green fields and houses, high-rise buildings and towers, and they meet many clouds too—friendly cumulus, shy stratus, brooding cumulonimbus, dreamy stratocumulus and a couple of tense mammatus. Those are in a hurry and don't interact much with the cloud-herder and his clouds.

The further they move away from human settlements, the more they come across wary clouds, who think this man works for a cloud-seeding company and will use an electric lasso on them.

For days they move like this. The old man drinks water from the clouds and eats his bars along the way, until, at last, they arrive at a place where there is only frozen land beneath them. That's where the cloud-herder spots his missing cumulus.

'He—ll—o,' he breathes out with some difficulty.

His throat feels rough and words feel alien. But the little cloud doesn't care, it rushes to envelop him in a fuzzy, lively hug.

Ever since he was a little boy, the old cloud-herder was accused of having his head in the clouds. His mind was always *elsewhere*. His thoughts flitted about like the clouds he loved so much. And his daydreams felt more real to him than anything else in the world.

About the time that he got married and then had a child, cloud-herding was only just coming up as a practice. But he quickly took it on and began to herd clouds alongside managing the farmlands he had inherited from his parents.

When his daughter showed interest in farming, he didn't think twice—he handed everything to her. His wife had long gone by then, and all he wanted was to live on a small plot of land with the clouds to keep him company and to take him floating wherever he desired.

They lay him down on the cold earth and hover. The clouds are afraid of what will come next. They are unsure of what they'll do *after*.
'It'sssss al—right,' the old man says. 'You all—ll go—ooo no—ww. No ne—eeed to—ooo sta—y.'
Slowly, he shuffles his body to lie on his back, with the view of the sky and the clouds above. He'd done the same a few weeks ago, when he'd come back from a doctor's appointment. He'd lain there, in front of his cabin, and called the clouds to him, to tell them what he'd been thinking.
The herd had pleaded with him, but he had refused to listen. Mind made up. So they had asked for a few days.
'Okay,' he had said. 'But after that, one of you will have to go.'

One morning, when the cloud-herder was about seven, his mother woke him up with the news that their family dog had gone missing.
'Gone missing?' he had repeated, still groggy.
'Oh, he's probably gone on an adventure with his friends. Don't worr—'
'He's gone off to die somewhere,' his father had interrupted, not looking up from the newspaper he was reading. 'Dogs do that, you know? They find a place away from home, when they feel their end is near. A very considerate thing to do, if you ask me.'

A kinder lie or a harsher truth. He wonders which version his daughter will tell his granddaughters.

It's so quiet out in the open, with the herd keeping watch over the old cloud-herder. The cold is a welcome respite too. He is grateful for the numbness, he has never been the kind to withstand pain.

He closes his eyes and opens them. 'Tha—aaa—nk yo—ooou, all,' he tells them. His herd will be free to roam here, far from the cloud-seeders and others.

The old man can feel death inside him now, freezing the life in his tired lungs. In the brief time left with him, he wonders if he has been a good father and husband, a good cloud-herder, a good person. He hopes, despite his failings, he has always chosen the right path.

He closes his eyes one last time, and the clouds above begin to shower him with snow, entombing him with their love. Memories merge and flash across his mind: the first snow he witnessed as a child, the cool shock of opening the main door on a winter morning, the clink of ice in a swiftly cooling beverage, the joy of dipping his head under blankets on an especially chilly night and feeling safe and protected.

He holds on to that memory for as long as he can.

Call for Kelp

Dr Fwish is staring at the screen on her computer. She is certain she saw an otter run past the camera installed in the woods. But her senior thinks otherwise.

'It was probably some other animal,' he says.

Dr Fwish stares at him. 'Shouldn't we try to save that too?'

'And what about the thousands of fish in the sea?' he counters. 'Should we get little fishbowls for them?'

She starts to argue but he stops her. 'Look, we're lucky they even allowed us to save the 249 otters that we did. Thank god that they're cute. But it's not possible … it's too late for that.' He points at the large clock on the wall behind them. 'It's only three hours to launch. How many more can you save?'

Dr Fwish starts to answer again, but his phone interrupts them.

She feels restless, wants *to do something*. But her hands are tied, so she longingly stares at the screen. Their little team of biologists and conservationists had only been brought in as a last-ditch face-saving exercise after a reporter had gotten wind of the fact that the testing of a super-secret bomb was going to kill thousands of animals in the vicinity of the testing site. Her article had drawn in a lot of protestors and other well-meaning individuals, and the military scientists realised they couldn't ignore this growing displeasure.

That was when a team of experts, including Dr Fwish, a conservation ecologist, from a nearby university was brought in.

On the very first day there, they were told to focus on the otters.

While the public, in general, was sad to read about the number of animals that would die in the blast, they were distraught to read that a large population of otters lived there, and that most of them would be lost due to the explosion. Videos of otters (not the ones at the test site) being adorable went viral.

In an ideal world, Dr Fwish would have been able to save them all. Actually ... in an ideal world, there wouldn't even be any need for a bomb. But they lived in a warped world, and she had to adhere to its rules and boundaries.

Or did she?

She stands up, observes her preoccupied senior, who is still on a call, for a few seconds and then leaves the room. The guards at the lab don't ask her why she's leaving, and she takes a detour so she bypasses the guards at the checkpoints. It was a much shorter route, narrow for military vehicles but big enough for her own mini hatchback. She had used this route before, for both official and unofficial rescues. On trips of the latter kind, she had managed to capture and release a few raccoons, foxes, mongoose, snakes, snails, spiders, bees, ants and a couple of birds about fifty kilometres away in the small, wooded area near their hotels.

She had used the Catchcaught cage to capture the animals, a device that, with a push of a button, released a net at an animal and encapsulated them in a thin bubble of safety. This bubble could then be easily picked up, put in a car or a truck and transported anywhere. Another push of a button, and the bubble deflated itself and let the animal out.

A marvellous invention, really. One that had helped her

on many field trips spent observing the natural habitat of all kinds of animals. It had greatly helped them in saving many otters too recently.

Unfortunately, she had left her Catchcaught cage back at the facility. And it was too late to go back now.

It takes her an hour to reach the spot where the camera had been installed. For a moment she doesn't know what to do. All her years of training and teaching seem to have momentarily evaporated in the midst of a situation that could, possibly, end in her death. But then she hears the klaxon call from the testing site, a warning that they are nearing the detonation time, and she wakes up. She looks around, crouches down, trying to search for the otter, but can't see anything moving in the bushes. She moves closer to the sea, hoping to see it there. Her watch is ticking away, and she is sweating—scared, full of adrenaline. She'll leave in five minutes if she can't find the animal. Just five minutes more.

There, she thinks she spots a tail. She leaps and almost catches it, forgetting all about the protocols of safety while capturing a wild animal. She should go back, but she is here, trying to save one more life. A part of her asks if it will even make a difference, but then she remembers why she chose this field, and how important each and every life on the planet is. Especially otters, her academic mind helpfully provides her with an answer, who have a direct impact on the population of kelp and help keep sea life in balance. So she dives after the otter again.

She can see it clearly now, running away from her. If it goes into the water, she won't be able to catch it, so she runs faster and faster. She almost catches the animal, but it escapes. It dives and hides, runs into dense bushes, slips away at the last second.

Dr Fwish doesn't know how long it goes on. But she knows that time is running out. Should she abandon the animal and run to safety? She can't decide.

She spots the otter again, and this time she spreads her arms wide and jumps towards the animal, hoping to catch any part of it.

And she does—she takes hold of one limb and three things happen at once:

1) The bomb goes off and the shockwaves throw them up in the air

2) Dr Fwish curls up and embraces the otter

3) The otter turns its head and bites her hand

When Saumwe opens her eyes, she sees a human lying on its back next to her. It's not moving, but she can't be sure that it won't wake up and cause her harm. On the ground nearby, there are odd markings that seem weirdly familiar.

No need to worry, a voice speaks inside her head. *My physical body is ... quite dead.*

The otter hisses in alarm and moves away from the human, but the voice still follows her.

I'm sorry to say, I'm inside your head, Saumwe.

'How do you know my name?' the otter asks. Her whiskers vibrate in shock.

You know mine too.

'I do no—Oh! Dr Fwish? But how ...?' The otter comes back to the human's body, scared but intrigued. 'What happened to us? And why are you ... dead? I remember you chasing me ...'

Dr Fwish finds it awkward to explain the absurdity of the situation, but she tries her best. *Well, you see, the thing is ... we, the humans, were testing a bomb ... and I was trying to save you ... I spent close to an hour looking for you, chasing you, and I think ... I took most of the blast. And somehow, I don't know why, our minds fused and I sort of clung on to your life force. Or, at least, I think that's what happened. Do you ... do you understand what I'm saying?*

'No,' the otter replies. 'Not at all. But I found a path into your memories when you were rambling, so I just absorbed everything that happened ... oh, wow.'

What is it?

'Nothing.' The otter pauses. 'Hmm.'

What is it?

'Nothing. I just realised we can't stay here.' The otter looks around. 'Radiation.'

Yeah.

'Is there anything I could do about your ...' Saumwe nudges Dr Fwish's still hand. '... body?'

No. No. Thanks for asking.

'And what's this?' Saumwe sniffs the markings on the mud. 'I think I can almost understand the ... words? It's coming to me now ... Does it say?'

CALL FOR KELP? Yes, it does. You were still unconscious, and I didn't really know what to do, so I—

'... called for kelp?'

Yes. My mind was mending, merging with yours. And whatever life force I had was trying to call for help, while my brain was telling me how important you, the whole lot of you, are for kelp ... you know what kelp is, right?

'I know. I just didn't know why it's so important. Climate change, huh?'

Yes.

'Yet another way you lot have ruined our world.'

At first they don't know where to go. But then Dr Fwish suggests they move south. There was nothing but cold and ice if they moved north. Saumwe agrees.

You don't seem angry.

Saumwe is running through the forest as fast as she can. They tried swimming in the sea, but found it difficult to navigate so many dead, floating marine life.

'Maybe I am. I don't know. I feel like my mind has opened, and the world is so much bigger than I thought it to be. I am still processing—oh wow, didn't even know what "processing" meant—I am still processing everything.'

Dr Fwish is quiet, still unsure if all is well with them, when Saumwe speaks again. 'Am I ... the only one left alive? My family ... are they ...?'

No, I don't think ... I mean, we did save many, you know. It very well could be that they're safe.

'So all I need to do now is go south?'

Yes, Saumwe. I don't remember the name of the places we relocated your lot to. And in any case, I'm not very good with maps and directions of any kind. She pauses. *I'm so sorry for everything.*

'It's not your fault, Dr Fwish,' Saumwe says, 'just the people you work with ... worked with.'

Hmm.

'Can I ask you a question?'

Of course.

'You are ... dead, right? You cannot go back to your body ...?'

I can't.

'But you don't seem sad about it.'

I don't? Hmm. Yes, you're right. I think ... I feel ... I don't know. I think ... more and more, I feel like I'm both connected and disconnected with this world. At times I'm horrified at what's become of me. I feel caged inside, I want to die. Again. Fully. But other times, and this side seems to be winning, I feel quite at peace. I exist but I don't. I see the world through you, and I see how beautiful it truly is.

It takes them five days, swimming and running, to find the first colony of relocated otters. But no one from Saumwe's family is there. Further and further, they move south. Saumwe draws on Dr Fwish's memories and expertise to make sense of the human world, and also gains a new perspective into her own realm—that of the non-humans—as they move along. She learns about things like 'NFTs' and 'car insurance', as well as 'burnout' and 'binge-watching'. And it dawns on Saumwe how blessed she is to be born an otter, living a simple life (at least until the blast).

On the tenth day of their escape from the test site, they chance upon a small gathering of otters resting on the coast. Instantly, Saumwe's entire body senses familiarity, and she runs towards her family. They embrace and greet each other amid squeaks of happiness. Saumwe tells them how she got separated from them—out looking for fish deeper into the sea—and how she found her way to them.

She doesn't tell them about Dr Fwish, though. She doesn't know what the others will think of her if she does. Dr Fwish sees her thoughts and agrees with her reasoning. *Take your time*, she tells Saumwe. *No worries.*

Later, when she is floating in the sea with her family—hands held together, all connected—Saumwe asks Dr Fwish if she misses her people.

A bit, yes. But not much.

'Oh?'

I really like this. Floating. In the sea. Not a care in the world.

'But there is *a lot* in the world to care about.' Saumwe feels an unwarranted amount of anxiety in her blood. 'There are wars and pandemics, and theft and murder. There are just ... What about kelp?'

What about it?

'Well, I mean, the whole climate change thing!'

Hmm. I'd forgotten about that. Well, there's nothing I can do now.

'But then—'

Shhh, Saumwe. Relax. Loosen your mind. Be with the sea. Be with your family. I'm just going to shut myself down for a bit, okay? I'm not leaving. Well, I don't know how I can. But I'm just closing out all thoughts. I've never ... I've never ... for a long time I have worried ... about myself, about the environment, about

Earth. I've never been at rest. I'm just ... [Sigh] I'm going take a bit of time off now.

'I ... okay.'

A while later.

Wake me up when you guys have clams, though. I had a shellfish allergy, so I could never enjoy that sort of thing.

'Hmm. I'm not sure if we'll have clams. I think someone said there were oysters nearby. Would that be okay?'

Oh, yeah. Absolutely! I've always wanted to try an oyster too.

Toothache

No matter how many times Jagat tries to smoothen the creases on his forehead with the tips of his fingers, they fall into place the moment his hands leave his skin. He tries to smile, baring his teeth in the mirror above the sink, but the wide grin, paired with his constant frown, makes his face look comical and, he is quick to note, foolish.

He'd woken up with the desire to clear the bristles off his cheeks, but now—with his mood quickly dissipating into a bad one—he doesn't feel the need to groom himself.

He has already brushed his teeth and run his hand through his hair once, so he leaves the bathroom with no other improvement upon his appearance. Jagat surveys his bedroom—the small TV in the corner blaring news bulletins on mute, the half-made bed he'll never finish arranging, two plastic chairs precariously balancing piles of his clothing. The chair on the left, beneath the only window in his bedroom, holds T-shirts, pyjamas and underwear that need to be washed, and the one near the bedside table balances all that he is yet to wear.

Jagat closes in on that particular chair, his frown deepening in thought as he clutches the neck of his red tee and drags it towards his nose for a questioning sniff.

'Hmm,' he concludes, a decision taken, and he picks up a light blue collared one.

Toothache

'Saab, matching-matching?' Darpan's amused voice calls out to him.

'Huh?' Jagat turns around, hose in hand, standing at the edge of his garden, watering his plants. 'What do you mean?' he asks the young man, who's waiting with a tray of toast, omelette, fruits, milkshake and cutlery for him.

'Your clothes,' Darpan says with a smile. 'They are both light blue.'

'Oh, that,' Jagat says as he looks down. 'Well, I ... I wasn't really thinking,' he adds, as he drops the hose and moves towards Darpan.

He takes the tray and brings it closer to his nose, to smell the mix of freshly cut apples and guavas, and the butter-soaked omelette. Darpan, meanwhile, heads inside, and brings out a plastic table and then a chair for Jagat to sit on and enjoy his breakfast. He also takes time to run to the side of the cottage and turn off the garden hose.

'Anything else, saab?' Darpan asks of Jagat, who has already gobbled up one toast and three-fourth of the omelette.

Jagat's mind creases in concentration. 'Have you thought about lunch?'

Darpan's eyes instantly light up as he excitedly declares he's going to make biryani.

'Biryani?' Jagat repeats. 'Do they make that here? I've heard of biryani local to Hyderabad, Calcutta and Delhi ... but never one that is made in the hills.'

'Saab, you forget,' Darpan says, placing his hands behind his back, rocking on his heels. 'I used to work at a restaurant in Almora before this. I know how to make anything a guest from Delhi might enjoy.'

'Okay,' Jagat says, with much doubt. 'What's the time now?' he asks, as he takes out his mobile and slides open the home screen. 'It's nine o'clock. Will you be able to make the biryani by two? Do you have enough chicken?'

'Of course, saab,' Darpan replies, smiling widely, for whatever he cooks for Jagat is what he himself eats as well.

Jagat gives him a nod, dismissing him, and watches on as Darpan opens the door to his living quarters—which houses a large kitchen, a small bedroom and a toilet—and steps inside.

Darpan may be young, Jagat surmises, *but he is very competent and knowledgeable.* He doubles up as the driver too when Jagat needs to go to the bigger village for some supplies.

Yes, he thinks, as he cuts another slice of the omelette, *I'm quite lucky to have found decent help—that too in the middle of nowhere in the Himalayas.*

He checks his phone again with his left hand, and notices the time, six minutes after nine. A thought enters his mind and he brings up the recent calls on the screen. His fingers hover over a name, he is not sure if she'd be awake yet, then abandons the idea and goes back to his breakfast. He leans back in his plastic chair, careful not to accidentally break it, and looks around at the green hills, the pockets of settlements and the ring of snow-capped mountains beyond. He smiles, calmed.

Jagat yawns so wide he thinks he must have swallowed a fly or two in the process. Belatedly, he places a hand on his mouth as he walks up to the main door. He can't remember when exactly he fell asleep; the last thing he can recall is looking at a few stock options online—buying some, selling others. He must have put his laptop aside for some rest and promptly fallen asleep. Ever since he turned sixty a few years ago, he was finding it difficult not to succumb to a midday nap.

'What is it?' Jagat frames the question as he opens the door. He knows it's Darpan on the other side, it can't be anyone else.

'Biryani, saab,' the young man promptly offers, presenting a casserole to him, like a gift.

'Oh,' Jagat says. 'Oh yes. Biryani. Will this be as good as the ones found in Delhi?' he asks, raising an eyebrow.

'Most definitely, saab,' Darpan answers, grinning. '100 per cent.'

'Hmm, okay,' Jagat says. 'Come back at five, we'll discuss what to have for dinner.'

Darpan bows his head and returns to the kitchen as Jagat closes the door and moves to his bedroom. He settles in, fluffing the two pillows behind him, placing the casserole on the bedside table, and picking up the remote to choose a film to watch on the TV. He finds a nice, generic action film to suit the role after a few seconds and sighs—relaxed and content to watch the television and eat biryani.

His eyes are trained on the screen. He's only looking down to see the kind of chicken piece he's putting into his mouth. If he'd been watching a calmer film, one not filled with as many explosions and jump scares, Jagat probably wouldn't have suffered in pain for the next few days. But now, the movie was chosen, the leg piece was near his mouth, and the actors on screen were about to be blown up in a grenade attack.

The moment the sudden boom filters through the television's sound system, Jagat's brain makes a split-second chaotic decision and instructs his teeth to bite down hard on the chicken. His eyes close in instant regret as the bone splinters and a small portion gets lodged between his canine and lateral incisor teeth, going so far as to press into his gum. And he knows, no matter how much he brushes that particular section of teeth, how much he tries to floss, the splinter will remain wedged between his teeth.

With his left hand, he clutches the overhead handle as the car twists and turns through the winding roads. And he places a gentle right hand on his mouth—as if that will stop the pain.

'Saab, are you okay?' Darpan asks, looking at him in the rear-view mirror.

'Obviously I'm not,' Jagat growls. 'Now are you sure

there's a dentist at Almora? A proper one? Not some pharmacist who ...'

'No, he's a real dentist, I'm sure of it.'

Jagat glares at the back of his head, trying to find a way to blame Darpan for his predicament. He breathes out a gruff sound and uses his left hand to take out his phone. He doesn't second-guess this time, and instantly video calls Aashna, who picks up after a few seconds.

'Papa, what's wrong?' she asks, concerned to see him covering his mouth.

'It's nothing,' he reflexively answers, and then remembers. 'Actually, no. It *is* something. I was eating biryani,' he says, glancing a glare at Darpan, 'and I got a piece of bone stuck between my teeth. It's even cut into the gum,' he adds, clutching his jaw.

'Is it ... very painful?' she asks.

He nods.

Her face contorts in empathy and concern, and then she narrows her eyes and points a finger at him. 'You haven't shaved?'

'No, well, I thought ...'

'And then you wonder why people think you look angry and unkempt.'

That is true. People do tend to say that, and this in turn makes him feel even more annoyed. He changes the topic, feeling that same irritation rise up inside him. 'You haven't called in a while. Were you busy?'

'Yes,' she says, her tone softening. 'Sorry about that. I should have called, but there were just too many deadlines to meet and I ... sorry, Papa.'

'No, that's okay. I understand,' he says.

There is a look in her eyes, and Jagat knows she's going to ask an uncomfortable question, which she does. 'You know,' she says tentatively, 'you could have called Kanika. She's stuck at home, studying for her exams. She would really appreciate some words of encouragement from you.'

'We both know she won't even answer my call. She is just like your mother.' He says the last word with unmasked disdain, which Aashna notices as she replies, quite sternly, 'You mean, your wife.'

'Ye—es,' Jagat says, taken aback by her displeasure. 'Of course she's my wife.'

And maybe Aashna feels guilty for admonishing him, or she feels sad about her parents' separation, because she looks like she's on the verge of tears when she asks, 'Papa, is there no way you two could get over your differences? Maybe if you apologised and—'

'No,' he cuts her off, his hand leaving the jaw, pain forgotten. 'No,' he repeats. 'Some people—like your mother and I—are better apart than together.'

She purses her lips in thought, and at once Jagat is reminded of the day he'd moved to the hills two years ago, when an exasperated Aashna had told him they shouldn't have gotten married in the first place. 'Sometimes,' she'd told him, with tears of anger in her eyes, 'I think it would have been better not to exist at all rather than see you both fighting all the time.'

But she says no such thing now. Just sighs, hunches her shoulders and asks him to call her once he's done at the dentist.

Jagat, feeling more upset than before, slides his phone back inside his pocket and holds the handle above his head once more. He glares at the vegetation outside, the shrubs and pines and wildflowers.

'Saab,' Darpan asks after a while. 'Will Aashna didi visit us this year as well?'

'Don't know,' Jagat gruffly replies, as the car runs over a particularly rough spot on the road and jolts them both. 'Drive carefully,' he barks out at Darpan.

'Sorry, saab.' Darpan pauses. 'How's your toothache?'

'Bad,' Jagat replies, as he places his right hand on his mouth again.

Darpan smiles as he thinks of something. He glances at Jagat in the rear-view mirror and asks, 'Do you know of Carpet saab?'

'Who?'

'Carpet saab. He was a foreigner, killed many man-eaters in Kumaon. I'm sure you know …'

'Oh,' Jagat says, realising Darpan means Jim Corbett. 'Yes. Yes, I know about him. I've even been to the national park that's named after him.'

'Did you see any tigers there?'

'Only paw marks,' Jagat replies.

Darpan laughs as he takes a wide turn, nearly spilling Jagat to the side. 'I've heard that forest officials make those marks with stencils.'

'Hmpf. I'm not surprised to hear that,' Jagat says. 'But why are you bringing him up now?'

'Oh yes,' Darpan says. 'Well, the thing is … he used to say that the most common reason for tigers to turn into man-eaters was toothache.' He turns his head and catches Jagat's dumbfounded expression. 'He said that the tigers used to be in such pain, that their teeth were so sore, that they preferred to eat the softer meat of us humans. We are also slower than many of their prey.'

'Are you saying I should do that too?' Jagat asks, amused by the information Darpan has shared with him.

The younger man is quiet for a beat. He shrugs and then asks, 'Do you know about the temple tiger? It was a man-eater too, and used to live nearby. Some people say it used to guard a special shrine deep inside the forests, that it was the guardian of that area.'

'A special shrine?'

Darpan doesn't answer at once. He slows the car to the

side and lets a truck pass by before he opens his mouth: 'It is said that you can atone for your past mistakes there.'

'Isn't that the case with every temple?'

'No, that's not it.' The car begins to move again. 'You can actually go back in time and change what you think is the biggest mistake of your life. That's what people say.'

Jagat scoffs. 'As if ... wait, what's wrong? Why are you stopping? Is that—?'

'A landslide, yes,' Darpan finishes and begins undoing his seat belt. 'I'll go and ask the workers over there, see how long it'll take them to clear the road.'

Jagat scowls in dismay. He'll have to wait for a long time now, or worse, return to his cottage. He tries to stop it, but he knows his belly is filling up with hate again. Annoyance at the world around, a deep irritability towards the people that occupy it.

'Well?' he asks Darpan once he returns.

'It'll take an hour at least,' he says, sitting down. 'Do you want to wait, saab? Or go back?'

'Is there a third option?' he asks as the effects of an earlier painkiller start to wane at that exact moment, making him close his eyes in pain.

'We are not that far from Almora, saab. You could walk up to it in less than fifteen minutes.'

'What are you saying?' Jagat opens his eyes in surprise.

Darpan points to the slope on their left. 'You'll have to climb that way, and soon you'll find your way into the main market of Almora.'

Darpan wanted to come with him, but Jagat insisted that he stay with the car and wait for him at Almora once the road cleared out. So now, Jagat has no one to blame but himself as he walks on an incline, resting his hand on trees once in a while, all alone on a mountain.

The pain in his mouth is sharpening to a throb, and he's

trying his best not to focus on that but where his feet land on the rocky terrain, when he feels the first drops of rain on his head. He tries to quicken his pace without losing his foothold. Then another fear strikes his heart: what if he comes across a leopard in the wild? There are no tigers in the vicinity anymore, they've been killed or confined to reserves, but there are still sightings of the dotted one.

Darpan didn't seem particularly concerned about sending him all alone. In fact, he'd once said how leopards only hunted dogs and fowls, and were quite scared of humans. Still, Jagat doesn't want to meet one in the forest.

Up ahead, he can see buildings not that far away. And he can hear faint sounds of civilisation, but the rain is growing stronger by the second and Jagat fears he'll be drenched by the time he arrives at the dentist's clinic.

As he rests near a pine tree, wondering if he can make a run for it, thunder roars above his head and startles him enough to make him lose his balance. When he rights himself, he sees a shadowy striped tail in the bushes right in front of him. His heart thumps wildly, he freezes in place. A fuzzy face peeks from within the plants, and then an entire tiger emerges from the fauna. Ten feet long, nearly three hundred kilos in weight, the wild cat looks like it could kill Jagat in a few lazy seconds. But it doesn't. For a long hard second, the beast stares at him before it turns around and reaches into the bushes once more.

Jagat follows the tiger, as if in a trance. He doesn't feel the sharp twigs as he heads deeper into the wild. His mouth feels numb. All he can do is follow the tail, which sways from one side to the other. They arrive at a clearing. There isn't much here, apart from an old, crumbling shrine in the centre.

He can't clearly make out the figure etched on the large stone, but the long hair suggests it's a goddess of some kind. While the tiger looks on, he edges closer to get a better look, and touches the surface of the shrine with an inquisitive hand.

At the back of his mind, Jagat registers the shaking ground, the stirrings of something like an earthquake, but he doesn't feel anxious or afraid. He is one with the shrine, the shrine has engulfed him, body and soul, and there is nothing to worry about anymore.

A yawn threatens to engulf his face and stretch his jaws to the widest limits as he opens the locks of his main door and comes face to face with the person who'd been knocking for the past few minutes.

'What?' he gruffly asks.

'Your biryani,' Darpan answers, casserole in hand.

'Oh,' Jagat says. '*Oh.*'

He stands there, deep in thought for the longest time. The safest bet, he knows, would be to not eat the dish at all, but then another idea strikes him and he takes the biryani from Darpan's hands and thanks him.

Inside his bedroom, he gingerly places the casserole on his bedside table and slowly sits up on his bed. He is careful to not make any sudden movements. Trying to keep his face relaxed, he lets the top row of his teeth sit gently on the bottom one.

This time, when he surfs the channels on his TV, he settles on the familiar, a film he's seen many times before. There are definitely no grenades in this one.

A Year (Not Quite) Alone in an Alien Wilderness

Loursge was two months away from being born when an official from the Employment Bureau walked into the nursery and drew an 'O' on top of the little ID screen on her womb-o-matic. A random decision, based on no logic. While everyone else in the nursery would be allotted a parent or two (sometimes three, rarely four), Loursge would grow up to be an orphan. Her job would be to take part in all sorts of dangerous missions—fixing the homeship from the outside, investigating incoming meteors, diving into black holes and fighting the more violent civilisations in the universe (whenever the homeship came across them). She would grow up surrounded by people all the time, in the sleeping dorms, cafeteria and training centres. And still feel quite alone, never quite connecting with anyone.

In her thirty-fifth year of existence, she would be sent out in a probing pod to look for a suitable home planet for mankind. Hers would be the thirty four thousand five hundred and twelfth mission to do so.

They weren't given any directions. All Loursge had was a map that showed all the planets and moons that had already been explored. Red crosses pointed out places with extremely hostile conditions or residents. Tiny outlined skulls marked the places where the prober had been confirmed to have died or, due to silence on the comm lines, presumed to have perished in the landing. Sometimes people attempted landing on those planets and moons, but largely, probers sought out new, unexplored realms.

Loursge has travelled a long distance, taking turns randomly, and now she seems to be near a solar system with five planets and twenty-five moons. She checks the display screen in front of her. Goes through the preliminary reports (which the pod's navigation system has collated using its surface analysing probe). One planet, Planet R2315, looks like it has potential. The screen suggests that it is oxygen-rich, has oceans and mountains. It is *green*. And is big enough to host what's left of mankind on the homeship. And yet, for some inexplicable reason, Loursge's eyes are drawn to the moon orbiting it. Much, much smaller, the satellite is all blue, black and green. Although Planet R2315 looks like it is full of life, its moon looks more inviting.

She steers her pod towards it.

Loursge wakes up with a start. She is still strapped to her seat, and the display screen is blazing red and blinking. A dark yellow holographic error message is swivelling and floating on it. For a second, still not quite conscious, she tries to touch the letters with her fingers, but her hand goes through the airy 'ERROR' and she hits a button instead.

Instantly, someone's voice now starts to shout that word from every corner of the pod.

'What the …? Why? Who is tha—' Loursge is now fully awake, and she scrambles to push the button to stop the voice from screaming.

Her haphazard, frantic hammering of the control board seems to do the trick, and the voice abruptly stops. Instead, the holographic message transforms from a single-word display to a soothing blue information screen. A soothing voice now reads it out.

'Dear Loursge,' says the voice. 'Please do not panic. Unfortunately, the pod has greatly suffered during landing, causing the comm lines to delink. You seem to have suffered too, losing consciousness during the entry. Such things happen, and cause a lot of discomfort. But you need not worry, the pod has enough food to last two Earthian years.' The hologram now shows her a pie chart of the various kinds of food bars in the kitchen (three drawers at the back of the pod, on the right of the shower drawers, which are full of body wipes).

Loursge is not a fan of this method of comm. She has been in crashes before, and the error messages have always been direct and to the point. This sort of personalised message is making her feel anxious. Despite the instructions, Loursge is starting to panic.

'It will take one Earthian year for the comm lines to repair themselves,' the hologram's voice continues, oblivious to her unease. 'After that, you'll be able to send all sorts of reports to the homeship. We wish you well. Hope you enjoy your stay!'

The voice stops speaking and the screen begins to glow green. 'Repair work will take 365 days,' the letters on the screen say, starting a countdown.

The first month, she sticks to the inside of the pod. She feeds random sentences into the movie generator and binge-watches senseless films. She eats small bars of food from the kitchen drawers. She sleeps to conserve energy. And she looks outside.

From every window inside the pod she looks out, noticing how similar yet different the flora and fauna of the moon are to the Earthian plants and animals on the homeship. There are vines growing everywhere. Blue, green and black. Growing on the dark blue trees, on the ground. The grass, short and neat, as if someone has tamed it, is the same colour. There are, what Loursge assumes, round fruits of yellow, orange and red hues hanging from the trees, and monkey-like animals that are in various shades of pink staring at her pod from between the leaves. She can also spot birds that look like eagles, ravens and owls. The only difference from the Earthian counterparts being that here they are all a calming mint green. All of them.

At night, she sees a multitude of luminous eyes looking her way. Lime green, lilac, fluorescent yellow, a dark velvety red.

On the forty-second day of her life on the moon, she dons a spacesuit and steps out of the pod. Carefully, she places her feet on the ground. She looks ahead and around, and feels innumerable eyes on her. Plants sway in her direction, and it feels to Loursge that *they* are looking at her too.

She is a few metres away from her pod when a great mass of pink swings between trees, lowering itself down the branches, to stand in front of her.

Shocked and unable to move, Loursge hopes the monkey's curiosity will quickly run out and it'll go back to hanging out in the trees. But the light pink simian, instead, reaches out and unlocks her helmet, throws it to the ground and exposes her to the elements of the moon. As a reflex, Loursge takes in a deep breath as she struggles to bend down and put the helmet back on. But her breath escapes and she ends up taking another lung-full of air.

More monkeys have joined the one from before. And they are all standing, staring at her. She wonders if they killed her on purpose, if they are going to eat her. But then she realises that she is breathing quite normally, and she is still very alive.

Her eyes widen and finally the monkeys do something other than stare at her. They bare their teeth and break out in infectious smiles that grow into hiccupping, echoing laughter. When that dies down, two of them grab her hands and pull her forward. Loursge doesn't know if she should go with them, but the blush-faced imps are insistent, so she lets her feet follow them.

Deeper they take her into the forest, where she sees multi-coloured mushrooms growing on trees, dark green deer, yellow rabbits with lilac eyes, peach-and-white wolves, silver and green tigers (Loursge tries to run away in fear, but is held back by the monkeys at this point) and insects in all sorts of fluorescent shades. Each new animal, insect and plant they come across, the monkeys stop and tell them about her. At least, she guesses that they are talking about her. No words are exchanged, no sounds are emitted. There is a lot of head turning and pointing.

It's only when Loursge is back in her pod—to eat some food—that she realises they had been communicating telepathically, and that everyone on this moon was *deeply* connected to each other. An odder thought is how the tigers didn't show any signs of violence, or any desire to eat her or the monkeys.

A few days later, she wakes up earlier than usual and gasps as she takes in the scene outside her window: the monkeys are all sitting in the clearing near her pod. Their eyes are closed, and their legs and tails are covered with vines growing from the ground.

She is not sure, but it seems to her that they are floating an inch above the ground, and that their entire selves are glowing a soft shade of yellow.

It's six months later, and she's running with the tigers, monkeys and wolves. She's wearing her always-clean overalls and shoes, so she is not afraid of the grey mud sticking to her footwear and clothing.

The animals were brimming with excitement when she had stepped out of the pod today. And she had instantly known that they were going to take her somewhere special. Although she can't understand every one of their cues, or hear what they say to each other, she can almost always understand what they are feeling, even the plants.

As she moves between the shrubs and trees, feels the warmth of her new friends, she realises how truly happy she is. She is glad to have found this perfect moon.

The animals slow down and so does she. Carefully they walk down to a waterfall surrounded by huge rocks. This is a part of the moon she has never been to. She can see fish crowding the surface, hoping to catch a glimpse of her. She can feel inquisitive eyes watching her from the shrubs and skies. And she can feel the pride and joy emanating from the monkeys, tigers and wolves.

She knows then that they have been waiting to introduce her to this region's residents for a long time. That they have let her feel comfortable with them first before taking her to new places.

As she settles down near the water, hundreds of tiny fish gather near. She looks into their eyes and knows that she is welcome. A few birds swoop down and stand on the rocks. Two of them directly land on her shoulders. Out of the shrubs, a silver-blue pig snorts happily and comes running towards her.

Later, much later, when she is back at the pod and has had yet another bar of dinner, she steps out and sleeps outside on the vine-covered floor for the first time.

Days ago, when she had seen how the flora and fauna of the moon consumed nutrients, she had thought that the vines were parasites, sucking the life force out of the monkeys. But as dawn had broken, she had seen the blue, green and black vines retreat, and she had realised that, though she was on a moon with life forms that looked similar to those on Earth, this was a much more advanced civilisation.

One year, not quite all alone, has gone by in the alien wilderness. Every dawn, when the sunlight is just waking everybody up, she meditates. She feels the soft grasp of the vines on her feet, feels the rush of energy flowing from the roots down below to the extremities of her body. When she opens her eyes, she feels refreshed and renewed, like a new person.

She can't remember when last she ate the food bars, or when she visited her pod. Days and nights she wanders the moon with the animals, she breathes in with the plants, she soaks in the lakes and ponds with the fish.

It is quite jarring to stand in front of her pod after so many months. It is now covered with vines, and is as much part of the moon as she is. As she steps inside the pod, she feels the gloomy moods of the whole forest—the wolves, the rabbits, the trees. For the longest time, she stares at the screen's hologram that tells her that the pod has been fully repaired, even the comm links. She only needs to reboot the system.

But Loursge just stands there, undecided.

To return would be suffocating. To tell her people about this paradise would be to doom its very existence. And to stay would be a betrayal of her kind, even though she has felt more connected here than when she lived on the homeship with the other orphans. But surely they'll find another home planet? Or maybe Earth would have rewilded by now? And they could return?

Her body stays unmoving, her mind sways from one future to the other. She keeps her eyes trained on the screen and the hologram as her mind absorbs the atmosphere outside.

And then she hears it.

It starts like the crackle of a radio. And for a second, she panics as she thinks that the comm lines have linked on its own. But no, the hologram is still floating in the air, urging her to reboot the system. She looks around, wondering if the pod is trying to read out a message again. But no, the sound is not outside. The little snippets (of what seem like) words are drifting in and out of her mind. They seem to be having trouble finding the right frequency.

She closes her eyes, still inside the pod, calms herself down and begins to meditate. She opens her mind, herself to the moon, and thinks back on everything she has experienced the past year. She begins to catch on to a lot of murmurings, but they are still quite vague. One voice is distinct, and it springs out—the voice of a shy, daffodil-like flower that grows fifteen metres from the pod.

Please don't leave. Please don't leave. Please don't leave. Please don't leave. Please don't leave. Please don't leave. Please don't leave. Please don't leave. Please don't leave. Please don't leave. Please don't leave. Please don't leave. Please don't leave. Please don't leave.

Half a prayer, half a plea. Aimed directly at her.

Sort Sol

There is a sort of madness, I suppose, in letting Shakespeare guide your decision to introduce birds of another continent, an ocean away, into the one you currently reside in. A scientific study would have been the sounder way. But Eugene Schieffelin, the man behind this unusual idea, saw the world differently. He picked through the Bard's works for every avian mention and used that as a reference when the American Acclimatization Society, of which he was the chairman, brought in European birds to the United States in the late nineteenth century.

Some took to the new climes, some didn't. The nightingales, bullfinches and skylarks he released all died out.

The starlings, which he set free in New York in 1890, couldn't care less that they were now citizens of an entirely different continent. The sixty feathery immigrants stretched their wings on that fateful day in Central Park and took off, travelling far and wide across the North American continent, which would, by the twenty-first century, be home to millions of their kind.

Sometimes I wonder how Eugene must have felt that day, and on the other days he released the Shakespearean birds in America. I wonder too if he saw poetry in his actions, saw a pattern where everything around him neatly fit into a larger cosmic puzzle.

Birding didn't come naturally to me. It was the result of weeks of depression and loneliness in the aftermath of my twins leaving for college. I would sit for hours in front of the television, watching it but not watching it, with a glass of red in my hand. When my husband came home in the evening, I'd have changed my position not one bit.

It wasn't just that I missed them or lacked purpose now that my nest was empty; I was unnerved by not knowing what came next.

I didn't want to get a job. I'd tried it a few times, and hated it. I didn't want to volunteer for a charity either. That I did on the weekends anyway.

'What you need is a hobby,' my husband told me one evening, taking out the bottles I'd finished in a week.

'But what can I do?' I asked once he'd returned.

He shrugged. 'Knitting? Reading? Trekking? Birding?'

'Birding?'

'Yeah, or birdwatching. You know ... where people go out and look at birds—'

'I know what the word means. But ... do you think I can do that around here? Is there ... a society, a group I could join?'

'There could be. You'll have to search and see.'

I asked a few neighbours. But they didn't know anything. I looked for flyers and asked my children to keep an eye out. And then finally, while I was checking Facebook (the only social media site I knew to navigate well) to see who all in my friends list had their birthdays today, I stumbled upon a small group for birdwatchers in my area. There were only twenty-seven people in it, but that didn't deter me, and I signed up for their next meeting which was set for a few days later.

I first saw starlings by the old pier that no one goes to. It has a few planks missing here and there, and exists only as a shell of a bridge to the sea. Next to me was the chairperson of the Birding Society, her binoculars hanging around her neck.

'There, do you see the black dots on the railing?' she asked.

'Oh yes,' I said, 'I can see them. How soon do you think they'll fly?'

'You won't have to wait long.'

And sure enough, a few minutes later, a mass of starlings took off in fluid motion, moving in an otherworldly current of air to form waves upon waves in the sunlit sky.

'Oh my—'

'Exactly.'

'Is there any symbolism in this? Are they ... are they trying to ... say something?'

'No, don't think so. But it sure does look pretty, doesn't it?'

When the twins returned for their first semester break, the three of us couldn't contain our excitement. My son told us all about computers, and my daughter spoke about how much she enjoyed learning about people and different cultures in anthropology.

'And you, Mum?' she asked me, smiling. 'How are the birds?'

'They're incredible,' I breathed out, proceeding to tell them about the swallows, sparrows, owls and, of course, the starlings I had spotted in the past few months. I told them how intrigued I was by them—how I had read every single piece of information I could find on them. I told them about the term *sort sol*, which is Danish for 'black sun', and is what the murmuration of starlings are called in that country.

The children listened, rapt, after which they both asked one after another:

'Why birds, though, Mum?'

'How did this even happen?'

'It just ...' I answered, 'it just felt ... right. As if this was the next ... step.'

After my children went back to college, I went by the pier again. All alone this time. I sat on a bench and waited for the birds to take off. I found the whole experience to be quite meditative—the lifting of feathers, all at once, all together. How often did we get to see such solidarity, such purpose in our lives?

I had my binoculars at the ready when I sensed a shift in the air. I placed them on my eyes as the starlings slowly rose up against the dying embers of the day and took form in four specific patterns: an O, an X, two Vs, one after another, and a dense ball of eclipse.

It repeated the same four formations again and again and again. It almost felt like a greeting.

Hello Hello Hello Hello Hello

My husband was dubious. After I had breathlessly described what I had seen at the pier, he frowned and told me, 'I know I was the one who suggested that you ... do *this*. But don't you think you're looking for meaning where there is none?'

I didn't think so. No. Not at all.

Still, I was hopeful that *someone* would show some support. I wrote about my findings on the Facebook page of the birding group, but only received a couple of laughing emojis in return. One ridiculous person even alleged that I had photoshopped the images. Me! The person who until recently didn't even know how to use Instagram, and was still quite confused by it!

A few days later, I was back with the starlings. I had taken a break to look at everything with a fresh pair of eyes. I wanted to be sure of what I was saying.

My phone was ready, my thumb hovering over the red circle for video recording, when again the birds flew up in the now-familiar pattern that I knew (for certain) to mean 'Hello'. Repeatedly it flew into that form.

But this time there seemed to be an extra 'H', followed by an unfamiliar shape that looked a lot like a human hand. *Hi.*

'So you two think it's a message?' I asked my children the moment they walked into the house for their winter break.

I had spoken to them over the phone and shared all the pictures and videos with them. Where everyone else had ignored my thoughts, my children had stuck by me. I really shouldn't have tried telling my husband or the other birders. Their minds were sewn shut.

'That's what it looks like,' my daughter answered.

'But ... but from whom?' I had asked.

'Aliens,' my son had offered, laughing.

'Come on, now. Be serious,' I had told him.

'Well,' my daughter replied. 'He is not wrong. It definitely looks like someone is trying to tell us something.'

I had been gearing up to ask another question when the disapproving voice of my husband jolted us from our discussion. 'The whole lot of you have lost your minds.' None of us had hear him creep into the drawing room, and were quite annoyed by the disturbance he had created.

'And why starlings?' he had continued. 'Why would they choose starlings to convey their message?' My husband looked like he wanted to say something but restrained himself and left us alone in the room again.

Half an hour ago, I switched on the television to watch some news. My husband and children are in the dining room, still eating their breakfast, but they can see the screen from there. The sound is clear to them too.

BREAKING NEWS

The television screams in red and yellow. The anchor is animated for once. His eyes are wide, his hands are shaking, and he is stumbling with words.

'Um, we are being told that ... I can't believe this ... but we are being told ... oh my god oh my god. There are ... I can't—'

The studio camera cuts off and the screen shifts to the shopping mall nearby, focusing on a truck-sized object in the parking area.

'What's wrong?' my son asks across the room.

'Is that ...?' my daughter says.

My husband is speechless, a spoonful of milk and cereal near his open mouth.

Some people are running away from the massive thing, but a lot of them are sticking around. Their phones are out, they are frantically taking pictures and videos.

A metallic thud and screech comes from the great object. A door opens.

Five beings step out. They are a lovely dark lilac in colour, with two arms and legs just like us. Their faces ... I can't tell if they have faces. There is a hazy, blurry mass floating above their necks. But their hands—five digits each—are stark and prominent, in a deep yellow.

Their hands move, fingers bend and curve. My children gasp and swear at the same time. My husband has returned the spoon to the bowl, but still can't *say anything*. I feel my heart beating fast, for I know what's coming.

All five of them bring their right hands forward and make circles with their thumbs and index fingers, then cross their index and middle fingers, next form a V shape with middle and ring fingers. They do this twice. Lastly, they close their fists, into the shape of dense balls.

There is a pause. The anchor has finally found his voice

and is describing how the object, their *ship*, landed out of nowhere.

Another circle with their thumbs and index fingers, then all three show their palms.

'We need an ASL translator. NOW!' the anchor can be heard telling someone in the studio as the beings take one last pause to complete their message: a repetition of their first set of hand movements.

I am suddenly engulfed by a hug on both sides. I can feel my children's excitement. My son tells me I'm going to be famous and my daughter tells me she's going to call the newsroom and try to get me on air. I turn my head to look at my husband, who is still sitting at the table. His eyes catch mine and all he can say is: 'I can't believe it.'

Ceaselessly Sea Follows

The sea follows onto lands overburdened with mankind and trees. It takes in a deep breath, a great inhalation, and then it follows. It comes in shapes of waves and tides, washes over inquisitive feet and drenched sand. And sometimes, on rarer occasions, it engulfs roads and houses, people and animals, hopes and griefs.

But still it hungers.

Inside, even in its darkest depths, it holds multitudes of living, breathing beings. They worship it, make it their home (even though they can't really go anywhere else), and for that it is grateful.

Right on the surface, there are ships and boats. People swimming, drowning and diving. They don't stay for long, until they do. They sink down to the bottom, in wreckages of wood and bones. Sometimes there is gold and oil, and treasures of all kinds.

And yet, none of it is enough.

So many things it possesses, so many things it has devoured.

But still, it longs for more.

One day, it knows, the balance will tip over. Already the icy north is melting and pouring into its watery grave. One day, there will be nothing left. And the sea will finally be able to gulp down cars, plants, restaurants, elephants, bridges, eggs, cushions, tails, clowns, wings, fans, whiskers, hair, skin, eat the Earth whole.

And then finally, it will be full.

Hunter

The car crunches over stray pebbles and uneven terrain as it slows to a halt in a clearing. A rugged man steps out, dressed in a red-blue plaid shirt, green cargo pants held up with a silver belt and blue rubber boots that have three glow-in-the-dark stars on the side. His face, impassive behind a forest of dark brown beard, turns to the left as he opens the backdoor and lets two dogs out: a Great Dane, entirely black save for a bright white spot on its forehead, and a Scottish Terrier, pitch black from its whiskers to its tail.

'Go on. Go ahead,' the man tells them as he reaches into the car for a fishing rod wrapped in its protective gear, and then closes the door behind them.

He comes here from time to time, to this riverbank in the woods, for a spot of fishing when the world feels too tiring. Usually, there is no one else here, and he stands knee-deep in water, stuck and content. But occasionally, he'll find other people—groups of friends, families, couples—and he'll do his best to ignore them and get on with his routine.

There is a group of four out on the banks today: a younger pair near the large rocks beside the river—the girl laughing and posing on a huge boulder while the boy clicks pictures of her—and an older couple resting on a picnic mat surrounded by food on the sandy lot—the man frowning at the sun despite a pair of sunglasses on his nose, the straw hat-clad woman looking at herself in her phone's camera.

But now she turns her head his way.

'Lovely day, isn't it? My daughter suggested we come here. Never knew such an exquisite place was hiding in the woods. That's her there, with her boyfriend. We'd go too, my husband,' she points at the frowning man, 'and I, but the stones hurt our feet. Plus, he's quite fussy about clicking pictures. Absolutely hates it.' She pauses as she tilts the hat up. 'My name is Cassie, by the way.'

'Hunter,' he replies.

'What an interesting name.'

He nods. He's thought so plenty of times himself. Of how violently he strives to be the opposite of it, becoming a vegetarian, adopting animals, being wary of guns and ammunitions. He could, if he truly wanted, change his name to something else. But it is, by far, the most important bequeathment from his father. And he can't let it go.

Just like he can't escape his inherent love of water.

Hunter moves into it now, his boots cutting into the stream, before he finds a place in the middle of the channel. There is no hook attached to the line and he needs some weight, so he bends down and picks up a small pebble from the shallow waters. He ties it to the rod with care. Behind him, he can hear the dogs running around on the sand, playing with each other. He pulls back the rod, like a whip cutting through time, then casts the line out to breathe.

He must have been around seven, or perhaps eight, the first time his father took him fishing. It was so long ago, he can't remember what exactly happened that day. Perhaps they caught a fish, perhaps his father told him tales about the land, all the animals around them.

On the other side of the river, he can see an odd little bird—a raven, or something akin to it. Its body is as dark as the night but for a few feathers on its wings that have a shock of white running through them. On his right, far away, there are families of swans floating aimlessly downriver. And when he looks back, Cassie is attempting a few yoga poses, and even trying a headstand on the mat, encouraging her husband to take an 'upside down' photo of her despite his reluctance to do anything of that sort. His dogs are occupied elsewhere. They have spotted a rabbit in the woods, and are currently staring (the Great Dane) and barking (the Scottish Terrier) at it. The wild animal, unperturbed and bored, turns its back to the canines to return to the depths of the forest.

And Hunter goes back to fishing.

When he was twelve or maybe thirteen, his parents took him camping to this very riverbank. They cooked food over the campfire, exchanged ghost stories and, most importantly, slept under the stars. The river water was so clear, and still is, that portions of the night sky reflected in it.

He can't see the stars in the sky now. Greying clouds are gathering, quickly blocking out a bright sun and all that lies suspended in space. For a second, he is taken aback when an object flies across it. But soon he recognises it to be an eagle, a messenger that heralds the coming of thunder and lightning.

There is only a light drizzle at the beginning, but that is enough for Cassie and her family to abandon their little picnic and run away. Hunter stays for a minute or two, but then the dogs start to bark in complaint as the rain gains in intensity.

'Okay, okay,' he soothes them, his boots leaving the river. 'Let's go. Laelaps! Maera!'

He notices the soggy sandwiches and paper plates on the mat to his left and resolves to get rid of the mat when he comes here next. Maybe next weekend. The food, he knows, will be gone by then, eaten by the pair of bears (mother and child) that lives nearby.

Hunter is so engrossed in thought that he nearly steps on a scorpion in his path. He recoils in terror—a childhood trauma, of nearly dying of a sting, flooding his brain—but gets over it quickly, and jumps over it.

The dogs are already waiting by his car, wagging their tails in anticipation. He takes out the remote, unlocks the car and opens the backdoor to let in Laelaps and Maera. They immediately shake themselves free of some water and curl up on the blankets set on the seat.

'You guys okay?' he asks them, wrapping the fishing rod and placing it on the floor, and they stare back at him with wide eyes. He gently closes the door and takes his place at the wheel. His mobile, in the glove compartment, is itching to come out of its coffin and speak again. And he must call his wife, Artemis, and let her know he's on his way back. But he ignores it for a few minutes more as he picks up the towel on the seat next to him and uses it to dry the dogs.

'Better?' he asks, as Maera cuddles into Laelaps's large frame. 'Hmm,' he determines. 'Yes, much better.'

He finally starts the car and reverses it out of the clearing. The greater dog is already snoring, its booming presence reverberating in the car. In the rear-view mirror, he can see the river receding further and further away from him. And he remembers being smaller and looking back, turning his head to glance at the river and the forest one last time.

He's older now, wiser and wearier. The wheels roll over mud and rocks, and he pulls his eyes to the path ahead. He can feel a tug at his jacket, it's caught in a hook. The line is strung taught, but he shrugs the feeling off and pushes on.

Cocoon

They have been driving for about two hours—through towns and villages alike—and Poltu has been talking for nearly one-and-a-half hours of that. Thankfully, he had taken a thirty-minute nap right at the start of the journey. But now there was no stopping him.

'Are you sure there won't be any dacoits there?' he asks for the fourth time. 'They love hiding in forests, don't they? What if they shoot us down, thinking we are government employees come to spy on them?'

Nilanjan clutches the steering wheel tighter.

'How many times will you ask me this question?' he replies. 'I've told you, there are no dacoits in the forests …'

'Anymore,' Soumitra finishes. He is staring ahead, sitting next to Nilanjan. He has the beginnings of a smirk on his face, a sure sign he is about to say something controversial.

'You know,' he begins, looking out the window. 'I don't think the dacoits are truly at fault.'

'What are you saying?' Poltu asks, gripping Soumitra's headrest.

'Their core idea,' Soumitra takes off, 'I get that. I get what it's all about. Sometimes, you have to use violence to make sure your voice is heard. Yes, some people think they are terrorists, but if I had been in their place …'

'I would have punched you and dragged you back to

Calcutta,' Arnab butts in. He has been sporting a scowl ever since he got suspended from work a few days ago.

Soumitra narrows his eyes at Arnab. 'Remind me again, what happened the last time you got drunk and started a fight with me?'

Poltu laughs and slaps Soumitra on the shoulder and then tries the same with his backseat companion, who catches hold of his hands and stops him.

'So,' Poltu asks once Arnab has let go of him, 'are you a hundred per cent sure there aren't any dacoits in the area?'

It is mid-afternoon when the four begin to walk deeper into the forests of Jangalmahal. They have dropped their bags at the guesthouse attached to the research facility, and only taken a bottle of whisky and a packet of cigarettes along with them.

'Is it a good idea to smoke in here?' Soumitra asks, dangling a cigarette from his lips. In his left hand he carries an old ashtray; his hold on it is light and loose.

'Who's got the lighter?' Arnab asks.

'We'll be careful,' Nilanjan says, swinging the bottle of whisky. 'It won't be a problem.'

'What if ... we accidentally alert ... others about our whereabouts?' Poltu nervously starts to say, but stops as Arnab hits him on the head and demands the lighter from him.

'Wait a second,' Poltu answers, rummaging in his pockets for one. 'Here.'

'I told the workers, the tribal women, to clear an area for us,' Nilanjan says, taking the lead into a denser part of the jungle.

'Tribal women?' Arnab asks with interest, blowing smoke from the corner of his mouth.

'Santhals,' Soumitra says, placing his cigarette inside his pocket. 'We met them outside the guesthouse while you were inside, still eating.' He stops and looks curiously at Arnab, as a thought lights up his mind.

Just then Poltu rubs his belly and belches. 'I don't know how, but city chickens just aren't as good as the ones found in villages.'

'I thought you were seeing that girl from office,' Soumitra directs at Arnab, who grunts and replies, 'Oh no. We are most definitely *not* seeing each other. She filed a complaint against me, said I was harassing her. And then they suspended me for two months. Can you believe that?' He hits a bush nearby as he says the words.

'I can,' the other three speak in unison, breaking into laughter.

Arnab glares at them as they move along, and then snatches the ashtray from Soumitra to stub his cigarette in it.

A while later, they reach the small clearing. A bright yellow bed sheet lies in the middle, with two solar lamps, just in case they stay there after dark, and four steel glasses on top of it.

As they sit down, the sound of a twig being broken fills their ears.

'Did you hear that?' Poltu asks, his eyes wide and his body taut.

'Must be an animal,' Nilanjan replies, opening the bottle.

'Or maybe ...' Poltu starts to say, but Arnab stops him.

'No, don't you dare,' Arnab says, wagging his finger at him. 'Don't you dare say there are dacoits nearby.'

Poltu scrunches up his face in protest, and begins to explain about how there was an increase in complaints about them and several skirmishes with law enforcement in the Jangalmahal area. Arnab listens to half of it before wrestling Poltu to the ground.

Soumitra and Nilanjan look on, grinning, and then the former turns to the latter and asks, 'Does your father know you've brought us along?'

Nilanjan pours two fingers of whisky into the glasses. 'No. I mean, he never directly asked me. He just told me to come here, check how the research facility was doing. But I'm sure he knows I wouldn't come here alone.'

Soumitra nods, scratching his bristly chin. And then: 'Is something wrong with the facility?'.

Nilanjan looks sharply at him. 'No. I mean, yes. The silkworms aren't producing as much silk as we'd like them to, as much as we expect them to. So the researchers are trying to figure out what could be causing them to get so ... lethargic. They have ruled out any disease being the cause of it.'

'It could just be climate change.'

'You think so?' Nilanjan asks.

Soumitra shrugs. 'So you ... grow tasar silk here? Wouldn't mulberry be better? Can't you change to that?'

'No,' Nilanjan says, as he hands Soumitra, Poltu and Arnab their whiskys, the last two looking glad for a break in this tiring conversation.

'Cheers,' they say all together, leaning forward to clink their glasses.

'No,' Nilanjan continues, 'tasar and mulberry are completely different. One belongs indoors and the other outdoors. Tasar is the one where the silkworms are let out in the wild, in this very forest in fact.'

Poltu looks around, swishing his head from side to side.

'The tribals keep the worms safe. They make cups out of the leaves for them to live in,' Nilanjan says, 'and when they build their cocoons, they pick them out and send them to the mills.'

'You know a lot about this,' Arnab says, a bit surprised.

'My family has been in this business for hundreds of years,' Nilanjan says, taking a sip.

'Yes. But still, we didn't think you actually knew anything,' Poltu chimes in.

'I am the ...' Nilanjan begins when Soumitra steps in.

'And how is the silk extracted from the cocoon?' He motions Poltu for the lighter.

Nilanjan frowns at him. 'I'm pretty sure you know.'

'But these two don't,' Soumitra says, puffing out a few rings of smoke. 'You may enlighten them.'

'Do you cut them open?' Arnab asks, already halfway through his drink.

'No. We ... uh ... have to boil them,' Nilanjan says. 'Only then do we get the smooth, intact strands of silk. If we wait for the moths to come out, the silk may get damaged.'

'So very cruel,' Soumitra says, nonchalantly, tapping his cigarette on the ashtray.

'It's just busi—. This is just how the world works,' Nilanjan responds.

Poltu shakes his head. 'So you just murder them?'

'You eat fish every day, and had three chicken legs for lunch today,' Arnab points out. 'Aren't you murdering animals too?'

'There's a difference between boiling someone alive and,' Soumitra slices his neck with a finger, 'killing someone swiftly, though.' He turns to Nilanjan, smirking. 'What would you prefer?'

Nilanjan gulps down the rest of his whisky in one go and fills it up again. 'I would prefer it if we talked about something else.'

The rest of the afternoon glides into evening without any further controversy. The only time someone raises their voice is when Poltu goes to pee deeper into the forest and comes back screaming, saying a neon green silkworm bit his wrist. Nilanjan asks him how he knows it is a silkworm when he's never seen one before, and the others just ignore him.

Still, they take the incident as a cue to head back to the guesthouse. Nilanjan is the only one to wake up on time the next day. He heads off to inspect the research facility and check with the scientists to see if there is any hope left in their work. In the afternoon, again they head into the forest for a drink before driving back to Calcutta that night.

When they meet next, twenty days have passed. They are at Soumitra's one-bedroom flat in Patuli, three drinks into their adda, when Arnab notices Poltu is eating slices of cucumber from a bowl.

'What's wrong with you?'

'What do you mean?' Poltu asks, mid-bite.

'What are you eating?' Arnab asks, disgusted.

'*Shaw-sha*,' Poltu emphasises the syllables.

'Leave him,' Nilanjan says, lighting up a cigarette.

'But I have never seen him eat anything green, ever!'

'Do you think you'll win a Pulitzer for this?' Nilanjan turns to Soumitra.

Soumitra laughs. 'Maybe.'

'I mean, it was so important you couldn't even meet us for half an hour these past couple of days? You just had to finish writing your masterpiece?'

Soumitra only grins.

'Where are you going?' Arnab's voice rings out as Poltu stands up from his plastic chair.

'I saw some apples in Soumitra's fridge earlier; I'm going to get one ... or maybe two,' Poltu says, moving towards the little kitchen.

Arnab instantly turns to look at Nilanjan and Soumitra. 'See! Something's wrong with him.'

'Maybe he's decided to eat healthy?' Soumitra ventures.

'Poltu! Eating healthy! He's more likely to be a ... spy or something,' Arnab replies.

'A spy?' Nilanjan asks, pouring some more whisky.

Arnab waves a hand. 'I couldn't think of anything else. But you know what I mean!'

Nilanjan nods. 'You are in a much better mood than the last time we saw you,' he states. 'Did they lift your suspension?'

Arnab smiles widely. 'Baba spoke to the CEO, told him it was a personal matter, so they couldn't really throw me out like that.' He picks up a cigarette from the pack on the centre table and lights it up.

'And no one can say no to the Minister of Education, can they?' Soumitra says dryly. 'Why did he wait so long to get you reinstated, though?'

Arnab leans his head on the back of the sofa. 'Wanted me to learn a lesson, I suppose.'

'And did you?' Nilanjan asks.

'Oh, absolutely,' Arnab replies. 'I'm a changed man.'

'I find that hard to believe,' comes Poltu's voice. He has returned with an apple in each hand.

'Wait a second,' Arnab calls out, delicately placing his cigarette on the ashtray. 'Come here, Poltu. Let me see your hair,' he says, grabbing his friend and pushing his head down to look closely.

'Do you see?' he directs the question at the other two.

'What?' Soumitra asks. 'Is he going bald?'

'No. Stop it!' Poltu weakly protests.

'Look here,' continues Arnab. 'His hair is turning green!'

'Really?' Nilanjan gets up to examine Poltu's hair. 'Yes, you're right,' he says, making Arnab let go of Poltu. 'When did you get it coloured?'

'*Why* did you get it coloured?' Soumitra asks, still in his seat.

'I don't know ... I just,' Poltu says as he hits Arnab on the head for manhandling him. 'It just happened.' He settles down, bites into an apple and looks on as the discussion veers towards Nilanjan's, or rather his father's, silk business. Apparently they are thinking of selling the business and starting another, one not focused on certain worms and their thread-making capabilities.

'What will happen to all the silkworms?' Poltu suddenly asks. Both apples are gnawed to the core by then.

'I think,' Nilanjan says, and pauses. 'I think the ones in the forests will just ... stay there. The new owners can do whatever they want with them. But the ones inside the research facility ... you know ... the ones being tested upon ... will probably be buried outside. That's the norm with any diseased worm or moth we may come across.'

Poltu's nostrils flare up, and it looks like he wants to argue, but what comes out of his mouth instead is a request.

'So, dear old Poltu wants to go to Jangalmahal?' Nilanjan's father states, his eyes moving over the newspaper in his hands. 'Again?'

'You knew?' Nilanjan asks, taking a bite of toast.

His father gives him a look. 'Why are you asking me this time around?'

Nilanjan shrugs. 'I thought I'd just ...'

'Yes,' his father says, folding his paper and placing it in his lap. 'You put a lot of thought into things like this, of whiling away your time with people like *them*.'

'Baba ...'

'Have you spared a thought for the silk business? If there's a way for us to save it?'

'Aren't you selling it off?'

'That's the last resort. And if it does happen, we'll suffer a huge loss. No one is buying into agro-farming these days. People are just using the land to build houses or apartment complexes. Have you ever looked at a newspaper?' he asks, picking up the newspaper and waving it in his son's face.

'Of course I read the paper,' Nilanjan begins, waving his half-eaten toast about.

'Your friends are just like you,' his father continues. 'There's Soumitra, who has this superiority complex just because he's pursuing a PhD in philosophy. Then there's Poltu, who has never held a proper job and is forever mollycoddled by his parents. Even worse is Arnab, who is spoilt rotten. I pray to god he never gets married and has children. And then there's you. You have so much potential, but you do nothing about it. All of you are in a little cocoon of your own, unwilling to get out and face the world.'

He glares at his son one last time and goes back to his paper. Nilanjan finishes his toast and walks towards the main door, lost in thought, used to his father's outbursts, but stops just as he is about to leave.

'So I can go to Jangalmahal with them?'

His father sighs. 'Yes, you can.'

Nilanjan isn't sure what woke him up. It isn't raining outside, nothing in the room is broken and all the windows are open. His friends are snoring, sleeping on their stomachs or their sides.

He frowns. Two of the beds were occupied, but the third is empty.

'Poltu?' his gravelly, sleep-addled voice wonders. And then, '*Ayi*, Soumitra! Arnab!'

They both groan in response.

'Where is Poltu?' Nilanjan asks, sitting up.

'Ba-h-room?' Arnab replies.

'No, there's no light from under that door.'

'Maybe the dacoits picked him up,' Soumitra says, which makes Arnab giggle.

'I think we should look for him,' Nilanjan says, already getting out of bed.

'Oh, he'll be fine. Go back to sleep,' Arnab murmurs.

'No. I just ... have this feeling he's in trouble. I can't explain it. He's even taken his bag with him. All his clothes are on the floor.' Nilanjan puts on his jeans and walks out of the room.

A few minutes later, near the door that leads to the research facility, Nilanjan feels the slumbering presence of Soumitra and Arnab behind him.

'What makes you think he'd be in there?' Soumitra asks, rubbing his eyes.

'Because the door is unlocked,' Nilanjan says, twisting the handle and moving in.

'Wait. What's happening?' Arnab is still waking up. 'Where did he even find the key?'

'I have a master key ... well, I had it. He must have taken it out of my bag,' Nilanjan explains.

As they enter the short hallway, with doors on either side, they all register the silence that greets them. They take a look inside each room through the little glass window on the door. And are nearly at the end when Soumitra asks if they should have been wearing gloves and PPEs. 'We are surrounded by labs, aren't we?'

Nilanjan swears. 'It's too late now. There's just one more room, anyway. We'll go back to the guesthouse after this. If Poltu doesn't return in an hour, we'll call up the police or someone.'

The very last room in the hallway is the most important one. It houses all the cocoons that are under observation for their silk strength. This is a quiet place, only once a day does someone check in on it. But now there are sounds of soft footfalls and hushed breathing emanating from the lab.

Nilanjan doesn't check through the tiny window. He opens the door and quietly asks, 'What are you doing, Poltu?'

The man in question, who is in the middle of gently placing each individual cocoon inside his duffel bag, freezes and stares widely at them. He tries to answer, but when he opens his lips, an interwoven network of web inside his mouth cavity makes it impossible for him to speak.

'Why are you chewing gum so late at night?' Arnab asks, moving towards him.

Soumitra stops him with a hand to his shoulders. 'No, wait.' He sounds a bit fearful. 'Look at his hair,' he whispers. 'Look how green it is.'

With a contrite expression on his face, Poltu wraps his tongue around the web and spits it out on the floor. Only then does he speak. 'I don't know,' he starts. 'I just don't know how to explain ... I don't think you'll understand. It's just so ...'

He places his bag on a table near him and moves towards his friends who, barring Arnab, take a step back. Poltu notices their apprehension and stops where he stands. 'Do you remember the last time we were here?'

Nilanjan nods.

'And I said a silkworm bit me, that it was glowing in the dark?'

'You said it was neon green,' Soumitra adds.

'It wasn't that dark,' Nilanjan says.

'What are you even talking about?' Arnab asks.

Poltu raises his right wrist and shows them a mark on it—a raised, uneven circle. 'I was fine the first few days,' he says. 'But then I began to feel this great hunger in me, and I couldn't stop eating any fruit or vegetable that came my way. The tips of my hair started going green around the same time.'

Arnab slaps his own cheek and opens his eyes wider. 'Is he making any sense to either of you?' he asks Nilanjan and Soumitra. 'Didn't he colour his hair to look cool? Should I hit him on the head so that he starts to talk normally again?'

'No, don't,' cautions Nilanjan. Turning to Poltu, he says, 'Go on.'

'Five days before we met again, at Soumitra's place, I searched the Internet for my symptoms. I thought I'd caught jaundice maybe or cholera.' He closes his mouth, moves his tongue around once more and spits out the web that has started forming inside.

A shiver goes through Nilanjan as he stares at the two globs of saliva-soaked silk on the floor. It all seems otherworldly to him, the stuff that fills up comic books. But he looks at Poltu, and can't ignore the signs that are pointing in one particular direction.

What is even odder is that, despite the growing nervousness in the pit of his stomach, he isn't running away. But then again, he is too confused to comprehend the reality of Poltu's situation right now.

'... and the next day,' Poltu is saying, 'something told me it wasn't a disease after all. But a new life that I was showing the symptoms for.' He looks at all three of them. 'Do you ... do you understand what I'm saying?' He nervously licks his lips.

Soumitra and Nilanjan answer affirmatively while Arnab replies with an impatient 'no'. 'Can you just plainly state whatever is wrong with you? And why are you here, stealing cocoons?'

Poltu spits out another silky glob and sighs. 'I don't know how to say this ... but I'm a silkworm ... Or man.' He falters. 'I guess ... I think ... Silkman?'

There is a moment of silence, then Arnab starts laughing uncontrollably. Such is his mirth that he doubles over and falls to the ground.

'Are you sure?' Soumitra asks.

Poltu nods. 'I've started making silk,' he says, pointing at his webbed produce on the ground.

'So that's,' Nilanjan says, pointing at his bag, 'why you wanted to come here? To free them?'

'Is that why you were roaming around the forest while we were drinking? You were freeing the silkworms out there, weren't you? Not looking for traps set out by dacoits, as you had told us then?' Soumitra asks.

'Yes. Yes,' Poltu says, his eyes shifting to Arnab, who is sitting with his legs spread out, still erupting into giggles every once in a while.

'Aren't you ... going to say something?' Poltu asks, anxious.

'In a second,' Arnab replies, laughing again.

'Are you ... okay?' Nilanjan asks, finally walking up to Poltu. 'I'm sure I could ask the people who work here ... to see if they can help you in any way.'

'Oh no,' Poltu says, smiling for the first time that night. 'I like who I am now. You know, I was going to rescue the silkworms tomorrow night, before we left for Calcutta. But as I was sleeping in the guesthouse tonight, I had this wonderful, beautiful dream.' He grins widely at Nilanjan and Soumitra, who has come up to stand beside them. 'I dreamt I was inside a cocoon myself. It was white and peaceful inside. I felt warm and soothed, it was just magical ... I don't think I'm explaining it well.'

'Go on,' Soumitra says.

'And then slowly,' continues Poltu, 'I came out of it. I picked at the threads till they unravelled. And when I emerged, I was completely changed. I was *changed*. I had these wings on my back. Brown with four white spots. I opened them, and they were magnificent. I felt *alive*, you know?'

He pauses, spits out some more silk and continues, 'Next I was on the roof, the one here, atop this facility. It was the most joyous thing to fly over the forests and look down below. I think I saw you three as well, in the clearing,' he finishes, with tears in his eyes. 'Have you ever felt something like that? Felt so complete?' he adds.

Before Soumitra and Nilanjan can say anything, or even hug him, Arnab slaps Poltu's shoulder and asks the other two, 'So, when are we going to boil him?'

In about a month's time, Poltu will find himself inside the research facility once again, in a secret room specially designed for him. He'll return to it every year when his hair starts to go green and his stomach asks for more fruits. Over time, his presence alone will boost Nilanjan's family business into profitability. Nilanjan will cook up a story about their increased productivity, and bribe a few officials to ensure no one from the government will try to snoop into their operations.

Inside the room, his entire body will lie wrapped in a silky, oval cocoon on a bed made specifically for him. And Nilanjan will stand at the end of it, waiting and watching the nurses carefully cut the cocoon off him. They will slice a straight line across his chest, all the way around, and take off the top half, revealing Poltu's face for the first time in five days.

'Hello, there,' Nilanjan will say. '*Kaemon aachish?*' And Poltu will grin, drag himself out of his body cast—first his arms, one by one, and then slowly, the lower half of his body.

Once dressed, he'll ask if Arnab and Soumitra are already in the forest, Nilanjan will reply 'yes', and they will walk into the clearing, a light brown coat covering Poltu's body.

Soumitra will see them first, and rush out to hug Poltu. But Arnab will remain sitting and ruffle Poltu's newly brown hair. The others will wonder about his tame response, only to groan in annoyance when he pulls out a solar lamp from behind his back and switches it on right in front of Poltu. The newly released man will struggle for a few seconds, harden his will and drag his eyes from the light and then he'll fly off in annoyance, promising to get back at Arnab one day. And Nilanjan and Soumitra will light up their cigarettes, lazily lie down on the mat and look up at Poltu flying in the sky. Arnab will laugh and call out a response, a warning.

'Be careful, don't go far. You don't want the dacoits to kidnap you, do you?'

Losing

Mrinalini gargles despite the pain, despite feeling like her throat is full of river-cut pebbles. She spits out the water and is hit with momentary relief. A feeling of warmth envelopes her. She clears her throat and tries to speak.

'He—hel—hello.'

Suddenly she is reminded of the many times someone has checked the mic for her, said a quick 'Hello, mic testing, check, 123, check, check' or a variation of those words. In the event of a malfunction, the mic was adjusted, the wires were checked or, as the final resort, the mic itself was replaced.

If only things were that easy for her.

An hour later, she is on the rooftop of her house. Dressed in a light pink sari and dark pink blouse, Mrinalini greets her audience, sits down among multicoloured cushions on a plush, soft diwan and closes her eyes.

Gathered here are a mix of people—a few members of her family, her students, her doctor and an official from the Weather Department. All of them have seen her like this before, but they still won't miss one of her performances (unless they are needed elsewhere). Each time, they are filled with awe and a little bit of fear when they are face-to-face with her abilities.

They are all sitting on the ground, on a dhurrie, waiting.

First, Mrinalini prays to the heavens above. She requests the universe for strength, feels herself connect with the energy all around her and thanks the Creator for her gift. Eyes still closed, next she draws in a deep breath, opens her mouth and begins to sing a tune of her invention in Raag Malhaar. She sings about greying clouds, dark skies, thunder and lightning, the first drops of rain, the smell of wet earth, and the joy and jubilance that the rains bring to the world.

True to the words that spill out of her, the clouds darken and spread above their heads. The boom of thunder, the spark of lightning crackles in the air, and the skies burst open with rain.

The small group of people gathered to hear her sing are under a well-used canopy, and are protected from the onslaught of rain, but they can't help but tear up at the spectacle in front of them. A great feeling builds up in them, and swells with hope as Mrinalini carries them over an ocean of possibilities.

Sumedha and Ritwik wipe their eyes and look on in wonder at their teacher, who has finished her performance and is now talking to her doctor and the official from the Weather Department. All three of them are smiling, exchanging pleasantries, but soon the tone changes and their faces take on a serious note.

'They look worried, don't they?' Sumedha asks Ritwik.

'I heard they're asking her to record Raag Malhaar for more and more regions, in a variety of languages. She's quite ... tired of singing.' He sighs.

'How do you know that?'

He shrugs. 'I saw it on Twitter ... someone was speculating that she looked more and more worn out.'

'Hmm. I see ...'

'I mean, look at her. She looks so ... drained. And the

other thing is probably true too. The rest of the world, those that can afford it, have been using all sorts of hi-tech stuff (all that goes over my head), but none of it is as powerful as *her*.' He softly turns his head in a nod towards their teacher.

'It must be extremely cheap too, to have someone sing their problems away. Even places that have suffered droughts and economic struggles can afford her voice. They certainly can't buy all those rain-bearing machines.'

Ritwik agrees.

None of the students can summon rain yet. They are only two years into a five-year study, and will start to show their talent in their fourth year. Only Mrinalini, a prodigy, had started to bring the rains down in her first year as a student.

So yes, there are other classically trained singers who can use their voice to control the volume, duration and spread of rainfall. But no one is as powerful as Mrinalini, whose abilities are said to be even greater than that of the legendary Tansen, the legend from the Mughal period.

It is a rare gift. And a great responsibility.

Mrinalini remembers a time in her childhood when the monsoons were enough. When farmers and others could depend on nature to help them survive. When newspapers and news channels would report daily, and in advance, about the rain-bearing winds. There would even be waterlogging and floods—an abundance of immense proportions.

But that world is long gone.

'Recordings are good. But they only bring rain for the duration of the song. And ... they need to be loud enough for the skies to react to the raag,' Leela, the Weather Department official in charge of Mrinalini was telling her doctor, Jai. 'The song she sang right now will bring rain for an entire month to this state—just enough for the farmers of this region.'

'But if she keeps singing live, one day or the other, her voice will break and her larynx will get so damaged that she won't even be able to talk.' Jai tries to reason with Leela.

She frowns, chewing upon his words. 'Won't she be singing for the recordings as well? How will that be any different? And ... and ... why can't we just record the live sessions?'

Mrinalini, who had decided to only use her voice when necessary, quietly turns her head to see how Jai would respond. In her letter to him, she had explained in detail why it would be so tough to convince the government about her decision: 'Every single government official I've met lives in the present. All they care about is how to use (or misuse) the power at hand. They don't care about vague things like the survival of mankind, or climate change, or the future of Earth.'

Jai looks like he is trying to control his anger. 'The recordings are a risk as well. And neither Mrinalini nor I know if she will be able to finish all requests. But the purity of studios ensures clear, strong recordings. And since Mrinalini can't go to *every* city and country that demands her live presence, recordings in the local languages are the best possible alternative. And no, singing in English or any other widespread language isn't a solution since a successful session requires that the language of the song be tied to the land, be birthed in it.'

'So she is not going to go on her scheduled tour?' Leela asks Jai, glancing at Mrinalini.

Mrinalini knows that the prime minister had hoped to accompany her on her live performances and reap all the benefits of it, use it to boost his image among the country's non-resident citizens. He wouldn't like Mrinalini's decision one bit.

Jai shakes his head. 'You could try approaching other singers,' he offers as consolation, but Leela gives him a pointed look.

'We both know they aren't that good,' she says, and then cranes her neck to look at the ten students sitting on the dhurrie. 'What about them?' Leela asks.

Sumedha will never say this to anyone, but she is quite sure that she is Mrinalini's favourite. Her teacher is encouraging, patient and supportive. But Sumedha can tell she is just a tiny bit more encouraging with her. She always, always, has a smile on her face when Sumedha is singing.

It's not something she takes for granted. Sumedha works hard—practises every day—and keeps an eye on the local weather reports to see if she's caused a sudden change in atmospheric moisture.

None of them can bring forth rain yet, but Sumedha hopes she'll be the first to do so.

Mrinalini knows the day is not far when her voice will leave her. For good. And what will happen to her country, to the world then? She wouldn't be so worried if any of her students had some promise. They were eager and hopeful, but none of them had *it*. Even the ever-positive Sumedha couldn't muster anything after singing for several hours in a day.

She leaves the official and her doctor to their discussions, and moves towards her students. Sumedha is already beaming at her, so Mrinalini gives her an encouraging smile, and asks her to sing something short and crisp.

And she hopes for a miracle, she hopes against hope.

People who have gathered around Sumedha clap as the song ends. It wasn't sung in Raag Malhaar, couldn't accidentally disrupt the rain. But there was a lot of yearning in her voice, which appeared to appeal to everyone gathered on the roof.

She waits in anticipation for her teacher's words. *Will she see all the hard work?*

Should Mrinalini fake her death and disappear? Leave the fate of the world in others' hands? Or should she try to make as many recordings as she can?

Entire families, societies and countries will be wiped off

the face of the planet if they don't get enough rain. Droughts are only increasing. So many towns have turned into deserts. So many lakes and rivers have dried up.

But what about her voice? Ever since people around her discovered her gift, her voice has been her only identity.

What is she without it?

'Good,' Mrinalini says, smiling softly. And then she takes her leave of the gathering, heading downstairs to her flat, to think some more.

Polarspeak

Above them is a swirling sky of green. As they walk, dragging their tired selves across ice and snow, Nanna's son, who is nearing three, asks how long they still have to go. Nanna looks back at those who have chosen to follow her into an unknown future and then stretches her neck to look at the sweeping, dancing Polarspeak urging her on. Their destination is not that far away.

Patience, Nanna, they tell her. *And courage.*

Nanna must have been around two when her mother had turned to her in the middle of hunting seals and asked her about Polarspeak. 'Do you know what they do?'

'They ... speak to you?'

'To me, and others. All those who have the gift of tongue can understand the messages that envelop the skies in the form of Polarspeak. *You* have the gift too.'

'Me? But I am only ... I'm just—'

Her mother broke in, 'When it's green, it tells us of a path we must follow, and what we can expect from the year ahead. When it's blue and when it's purple, it tells us that happiness will surely follow. And when it's red, a cold, dark red, it warns us of the grief and danger that will stick to us like frost for a long, long time.'

Nanna didn't know what to say. 'But how will I

understand the message itself? Will you ... teach me?'

Her mother shook her head. 'That is something that will come to you with time. You cannot ask others for help in interpreting, for it may influence the way your mind works. Now, come along, we must eat,' she had said, glancing at Nanna. 'Later I need to ask you something important.'

That night, the sky had turned a mix of green, blue and red. And her mother, shivering despite the warm coat of fur, had looked up for hours on end, at the end of which she told Nanna that she was a child no longer.

'From now on, till the end, you will have to fend for yourself, all on your own.'

'Do you even know where you are going?' Egil, an old male who has ambled up to her, asks her.

'Do you doubt the skies?' Nanna replies.

'No.' He bares his teeth in a grin. 'I don't doubt *that*. But interpretation ... messages can be lost in them, can't they?'

Nanna takes a quick look at her son, who is now walking with the other young ones, a few paces behind. 'If you want to go back, you can,' she tells Egil. 'I'm not going to stop you.'

'There is no need to be rude,' he replies, turning around and heading back to his position in the group. 'I was just checking if you knew where you were going.'

He isn't the only one. From time to time, the others come up to her with questions filled with anxiety, doubt and a bit of disdain for her role as the leader. But the one she truly wants to speak to remains at the end of the line, elusive and aloof.

'Am I making the right decision?' Nanna had asked at the Great Gathering.

Her mother, whom she hadn't seen for the past ten years, had only nodded and said, 'Come along now, they are waiting.'

It had taken Nanna an entire year to understand the ways of Polarspeak.

One of the first things they told her was that she had an important task, and that her future was foretold the night Nanna's mother drove her away. They also told her where the most seals were, and where to sleep unperturbed. How to stay away from those who might hunt them, how to stay alive.

And during a very cruel winter, when several of her kind died of starvation, the Polarspeak asked her to prepare for a gruelling journey that would determine the future of their entire species.

'But remember, Nanna,' they had told her. 'It will all come at price.'

Up ahead, they can see the research ship now. The humans, so small in stature, are only dots of black and red and green. A wave of excitement flows through the group at the sight, as does an outpouring of apprehension, despair and disdain.

'Are you sure they will take us on board?'

'What if they kill us?'

'How sure are you that they aren't responsible for the situation we are in?'

It's Egil who asks this question, which is a repeat of what he had pestered her about at the Great Gathering a few months ago. She had told him then what she tells him now: 'Would you rather starve to death?'

His nose scrunches in anger, but before he can do anything else, Nanna's mother walks up to them and nudges Nanna with her nose.

'It's time.'

'Are those ... are those polar bears?' a bearded man asks. 'There are hundreds of them!'

'No, no, no, no, no,' another man keeps repeating.

'There are hundreds of them,' the youngest of the humans softly says.

'What should we do?' the bearded man adds.

Before they can come to a decision, a mother and child approach the group. The female, who seems to be leading the group, extends her snout towards the bearded man, frozen in place, and sniffs his gloved hands. She turns her head and gives an imperceptible nod, and moves towards the stairs leading to the research ship.

As the humans look on, in wonder and shock, slowly and steadily, hundreds of polar bears climb the vessel and take up space on and below the deck.

'What have you learnt in the past two years, Nanna?' her mother had asked. 'What is of the utmost importance in our lives?'

'Seals?'

'Close,' her had mother answered. 'Think broader, think again.'

Nanna had taken some time to arrive at an answer. 'Survival?' she had asked after a few minutes.

Her mother had nodded her head. 'Survival,' she had confirmed. 'No matter what.'

Corvid Inspector

Bram

Funerals have never elicited any emotional response in him. As the Corvid Inspector in charge of investigating suspicious injuries and death, Bram has come across many gruesome sights: ravens with broken wings, treepies dead due to human negligence, jays traumatised and clawed by cats. And yet, lately, he's been feeling weighed down. The sight of a bird lying on its back, its legs in the air, in a secluded area of Oak Shadow Park is making him crave the comfort of the nest he grew up in.

Ciara, the black-billed magpie, has already spoken words into the wind and prayed for the departed soul. Around her are members of the dead crow's family, their heads are bowed and eyes closed. Bram walks towards them, feathers ruffled in discomfort, unsure how to interrupt them. But then one of them, the mother, feels Bram's presence and looks up at him, accusation quickly colouring her gaze.

'What are *you* doing here?' she asks.

'I'm the CI,' Bram answers in a neutral croak.

'Ma is asking why they couldn't send someone else,' says Cornell, the brother of the victim, a middle-aged crow, moving towards Bram. 'You can't be the only CI.'

'I am.'

'I highly doubt that.'

'Do you want some dumb pigeon here? Or a sparrow?' Bram snaps.

The brother's eyes narrow in anger. The others have stopped praying and are now looking at the two of them. 'You're really happy, aren't you?' Cornell says. 'Real happy that one of us is dead?'

'Don't be absurd.'

'Sure, crows and ravens have all sorts of territory disputes,' Cornell continues, 'but your father … yes, I remember him … your father took it a step too far—'

'Not that again,' Bram starts. 'Listen, it was just a job—'

'He took away our home!' Cornell caws at him, loudly.

Bram moves closer to him and opens his beak in a warning. 'Your *landlord* mortgaged the entire tree, all the nests inside it and then found that he could not pay the amount. All my father did was work for the bank. He had no ill intentions towards you or anyone. He was just doing his job. Does your small brain understand that?'

'You know,' Swift, the victim's daughter who has walked up to him says, 'you don't have to be so rude. We are in mourning, and have no idea who could have done this to Dad. We don't know if it was an accident, or if he was murdered. You don't have to behave in this way.'

'Oh yeah?' Bram asks. He can't control his irritation now. 'So your uncle will say just about anything and I'll have to listen?'

'You can still be a little understanding.'

'Why? Why do *I* have to be understanding? Why do I have to adjust?'

'Because you have suffered as well … even more than us.'

'Listen, fledgeling,' Bram says, hating the direction the conversation has suddenly taken. 'You and I both know the kind of crow your father was. He probably had it coming.'

'How dare you—' the brother starts, but the young crow edges up to him, pushing her uncle out of the way. 'The humans were right about you lot,' she says. 'An unkindness of ravens ... that's what they call a group of you, isn't it?'

'Is that right?' Bram says, unable to stop himself from saying the next words. 'And what do they call a group of crows?'

As Bram flies towards the police grove, he feels tired. And it's only eight in the morning. He hasn't been sleeping well the past couple of days. He woke up with grass in his feathers again this morning, but hasn't had time to clean them yet. He is now a sour, irritable corvid.

The altercation at the funeral has only added to his dour mood. The one reason he escaped the claws and beaks of the grieving family was because the daughter beat her wings at him and told him to 'leave at once'.

Maybe he shouldn't have said those things. Maybe he shouldn't have taken up this case. Maybe what he should have done is taken early retirement and just flown away.

But here he is now, swooping in to settle down on his branch on the grand oak tree, the Department of Corvid. The Daurian jackdaw and the western rook, who look after petty crime, are sitting in their usual spot on the branch under him.

Bram used to have a partner too, a crow who was his senior and used to take charge of murders and suspicious deaths. But she retired a year ago, and went to live in the nearby woods, away from human chaos.

'Have you met the new one?' Nyx, the jackdaw, suddenly asks him, elegant in the way she picks up her wings and flies up to sit next to him.

'The new what?'

'The new recruit who's going to work with you. I haven't really spoken to her, only said a chirpy hello. But she's a New Caledonian crow as far as I could tell. Oh—' Nyx stops, spotting two pairs of wings coming towards them from afar. 'Here she comes, with Polly in tow.'

A flap of wings and the jackdaw is back in her spot.

Bram can't say he likes Polly, the chief. Light grey and white-faced, she has the unfortunate tendency to parrot back the words of her superiors. She never once tried to intervene on his behalf, never once tried to understand his point of view. She only knew how to follow the mayor's instructions.

'All okay, Bram?' Polly asks. She perches right beside him, with the newcomer on her left.

'Saw that damn dead crow to—. Sorry,' he says, immediately realising his mistake. 'I didn't mean to sound so rude. It just came out.'

Polly looks disapprovingly at him, and also apologises to the New Caledonian. 'Don't mind him,' she says, then whispers loudly, 'He has been through a lot.'

Bram involuntarily lets out an annoyed croak, which makes Polly jump.

'Anyway, I just wanted to introduce you two to each other. Birdie, this is Bram. Bram, this is Birdie. She will assist you on your cases from now on.'

'Hey!'

'Hi.'

And because he can't control his tongue, Bram adds, 'Does her recruitment have anything to do with the mayor's upcoming campaign? The crows aren't too happy with him since he raised the real estate tax. Her kind control the land and provide construction supplies for most nests.' He adds that last bit for Birdie.

'I've heard that his opponent is a snake,' Birdie replies and Bram's eyes quickly flash to her. *How did she know?*

Polly seems to have the same thought, but rather than feeling suspicious, she relishes the fact that he seems stumped. 'Now, now, let's not discuss politics. Update Birdie on the case. Okay, Bram? And take her with you to the interview.'

'What interview?'

Polly frowns at him as she readies to fly off to the upper branches to her own office. '*What interview!* Well, you have to talk to the victim's family and acquaintances, don't you?'

The dead crow, Corvus, used to own a restaurant near the garbage dump. Bram didn't go there often. He almost always ended up in a fight with a crow when he went there, but they had the cheapest worms, berries and carcasses in town, and sometimes he was just too lazy to go hunt on his own.

Bram was hoping to talk to the employees and get over with it, but of course he had no such luck.

'Again?' the victim's daughter asks as Bram and Birdie land at the restaurant. 'Did you want to insult us further?' Her eyes move to Birdie. 'Who are you?' she asks, accusingly, but in a softer tone than the one she used for Bram.

'I'm Birdie, I'm his new partner.'

'Well, then I feel sorry for you.'

Birdie laughs with a squawk. But then she straightens up and apologises, 'I'm so sorry for your loss.'

Swift nods her head.

'We will try our best to figure out what happened to him.'

Swift sighs. 'He died once before, you know,' she says, looking only at Birdie and ignoring Bram. 'He got tangled up in electric wires and didn't have a heartbeat for a few seconds. But some good humans saw him and brought him back to life.'

'That must have been awful,' Birdie says sincerely.

Swift lets out a sudden sad caw. 'It was ... And now ... now ... he—'

'There, there,' Birdie comes over and envelops her with her wings as Bram watches the entire scene, dumbstruck.

Later, when they are about to leave, the daughter thanks Birdie and tells her she is not surprised at her kindness.

'You know,' she says, 'we are friends with a lot of New Caledonians, and they are all so sweet. Except the one who was our la—'

'Is that right?' Birdie interrupts. 'How lovely. But I'm sorry now, we have to go back to the station. Will you be fine?'

'Yes, thank you. Of course, go ahead. I won't keep you here.'

'You're very good at that,' Bram begrudgingly tells Birdie when they are in the air.

'Oh I'm just being polite, you know?'

'Hmm. So ... do you have any ideas?' Bram asks casually. 'What could have killed him?'

'It's too early to say. There are still so many birds to interview. Maybe it was a family issue, a rivalry, or maybe it was a property dispute?'

'Hmpf.'

'You don't think corvids can be killed over property?'

'They can ... but not him. I have a sense about these things, and it just ... doesn't seem right.'

They are flying over a park now, a park where Bram used to live not that long ago. He stiffens as he recognises it, and Birdie notices his discomfort. 'I'm sorry, by the way. I heard about ... you know. I was in Magnolia Park, getting ready to leave my roost, when that happened. I didn't want to say anything when we met, but—'

'Then don't!' Bram snaps as he picks up speed.

An unflustered Birdie lands on a roadside tree only a few seconds after he does. They are here to meet a spotted nutcracker who was fired from the victim's restaurant only a few days ago. The daughter had said a fierce fight had followed when her father had refused to increase his pay. The nutcracker had threatened the victim, told him he'd burn him and his restaurant and then flown away.

'I'm glad he's dead,' Domino, the spotted nutcracker says, unprompted. He is sitting on a branch, looking quite tired. 'He was absolutely the worst boss I ever had. Rotten to the core.'

'Are you admitting it then?' Bram asks. 'You killed him?'

Domino squawks. 'I wish I had. But no, I was at a build site the last three days. It was a last-minute job, so I couldn't take any breaks. You can check with the couple I built the nest for if you don't believe me.'

'I don't. And we will,' Bram says, preparing to leave.

Birdie is not yet done, it seems. She stays put and asks Domino if there was anyone he'd seen the victim fight with.

'So many birds—employees and customers, even the landlord. So many fought with him.' He pauses, thinking. 'But there was one bird that would turn up at night. He or she would fly haphazardly, half in air half on land, and bump into us. We never saw their face clearly, there is hardly any light near the restaurant. Once or twice they hit the Boss too, and he got really angry, tried to claw at the mysterious bird, but it flew away.'

'Why didn't he file a complaint about this?' Bram asks.

The nutcracker shrugs his feathers. 'So many despised the Boss. He didn't think a complaint would actually lead anywhere.'

'Hmm ... and this bird who attacked him, do you remember anything about them?'

'Too dark.'

'But what size? Someone like the CI or bigger?'

'Definitely near the CI's size,' Domino answers.

'That was a very pointed question.'

'Which one?' Birdie asks. They are now standing at the base of a dying tree, waiting for the carrion crow to call them inside.

'The one about the mysterious attacker's size?'

'Oh, that. Well, you were right there,' she says. 'Who else could I have mentioned for a comparison?'

'Hmm.'

'I'm sorry, by the way, Bram—about before, when we were flying over that park.'

'Then stop mentioning it.' He is in a really bad mood. He can sense that things are not right, that Birdie is no ordinary recruit. He has a feeling that the mayor has a hand in this, that he wants to do away with Bram. They had never seen eye to eye, and that had only deteriorated when—

'Come on in,' Merle, the carrion crow, calls from within, and the two step inside the hollow. There is a dead dwarf jay right in the middle of the corvid-doctor's office.

'Just dropped dead while flying, this one,' Merle says. 'I needed to investigate what was wrong with him.'

'So what was it?' Bram asks.

'Not too sure about that… yet,' she replies. 'Now, let's talk about your case. The victim is a crow, middle-aged restaurant owner, frequent fighter and instigator. I saw his body. Couldn't bring it here since the family didn't allow it, but I did see the body.'

'And?' Birdie asks.

'The weapon that caused the injuries had a sharp, strong point. Could be a beak or a metal wire, anything. If I get the chance to examine the body more thoroughly, I'll be able to tell you for sure.'

'Is that what killed him, though?' Bram asks. 'Were the wounds deep enough?'

'No,' Merle says. 'No, they weren't. But the attack might have startled his heart and … did he have a heart problem?'

'His daughter said he had been electrocuted once, and his heart had stopped beating,' Birdie says.

'Well, there you have it,' Merle says.

'You know,' Birdie says softly. 'I understand your pain.'

'Oh, really?' Bram answers, tired. They are back at the police station, sitting on their assigned branch.

She nods her head. 'I was only a few days old when my parents died. I don't even remember what they looked like.'

Bram turns his head to look at her, but she's looking at the branch below, almost transfixed by the magpie, Ciara, who's complaining about her stolen cache of nuts and seeds.

He knows he should say he is sorry, and apologise for his behaviour earlier. But his mind is elsewhere too.

'You know,' he says quietly, 'it's been a long time since I've seen them in pairs.'

Late at night, he stumbles into Elm Grove Park, where he used to live before. He sees broken anthills under a massive tree and hops over to them. He sees several ants, selects five with his bill and rubs them all over his wings to clean his feathers—and, more importantly, to feel numb. It only takes a second after that, to feel the effects of ... nothing.

There are no thoughts in his head, no feelings or doubts. He walks toward something, and he can't tell if it's a rock or a bird.

It's an old blue jay. 'Are you okay?'

'Wha—?' Bram answers, eyes drowsy, feet unstable. He shouldn't have taken so many ants, a voice at the back of his head tells him.

'I live nearby, and I've seen you here the last couple of nights anting up the place. Most nights you're sad, other nights you are quite angry and itching for a fight. Are you ... okay?'

'Meb-bie yeah-hh.'

'You don't seem well. Is there anyone I could call?'

Bram falls to the ground and rolls around in the grass. He sees the sky above, so vast and unending.

The jay keeps asking questions, but Bram only stares at the heavens above. *When did it get so dark?* he wonders.

One month ago, he had a partner and three eggs just about to hatch. They were so happy, so carefree. And then, one day, he was away for work and a bunch of visiting owls came to the park and attacked the nest, killing the lives growing within it. A bystander saw it and reported the crime. But no one took down his or her details, and they could not be contacted again.

As much as Bram tried to question everyone to figure out who the owls could be, he never got anywhere with the case. The mayor and the chief refused to help beyond a point, citing potential tension within the avian community for targeting the owls over an anonymous bird's report.

A few days after the death of his unborn children, his partner, lost in grief, didn't pay attention while flying through human settlements and crashed into a large glass building, dying a few days later.

Bram can feel the stares of every bird on the tree when he turns up late to the old oak. He wonders if he has ants on his feathers or grass stuck between his beak. Instead, Polly takes him aside to a nearby tree and tells him that the mayor had turned up, angry that the case still hadn't been solved, and asked Birdie for initial reports.

'I'm sorry, Bram,' the chief says, 'but every single clue she pointed out seemed to be aimed at you ... And everyone heard it.'

'What are you saying?'

Polly ruffles her feathers in nervousness. 'The mayor suggested that we put you on leave for a few days, maybe a month. Just ... just in case, this blows up. It won't of course, we will try our best to soothe the crows. But you never know ...'

'But I didn't do anything, Polly! How can you just believe what Birdie is saying? She is *obviously* working for the mayor ...'

'Oh come on, Bram!'

'No, you listen to me! I'm being framed ... Why would I kill that damn crow? I don't even know him that well!'

'You don't,' Polly answers softly. 'But you are grieving, you are angry and you have been anting for the past couple of days because of that—oh yes, I noticed—and who knows what you could have done? You might have visited the restaurant too.'

'But, Polly. You *know* I couldn't have done this!'

'I do. But just to be safe, Bram. And for your own mental health, please take a couple of days off and rest at home?'

But he doesn't have a home. These days he either roams around, high on ants, or he selects a random tree and sleeps there for the night. His only true home is with his dad, Bertram, who lives half an hour away in a wooded area.

He flies there now.

Over the parks and buildings, cars and humans walking around. There are birds who fly past him, too busy and in a rush to engage him in a conversation—not that he's in a chatty mood.

It takes him a while to figure out his father's tree. He checks a few walnut trees before he sees his father staring at him from a mahogany one, looking amused.

'What are you doing?' Bertram asks.

'I am looking for you,' Bram says, flapping his wings to reach him.

'I'm not surprised the old crow died like that,' his father says. 'He got into *a lot* of fights. Once, someone pushed him into electric wires and he died on the spot. A kind human saw him and brought him back to life.'

'Someone pushed him?' Bram asks. 'Do you remember who?'

'No, I don't. I heard it from a friend of mine. But I remember how feisty he was. When their landlord lost them their tree, the entire family was fighting every day over it, looking for someone to blame.'

'They didn't blame the landlord?'

'Oh, they did. He was a New Caledonian, a new father too. And so many birds were after him back then that he killed his partner and himself. Drove themselves right into a flying airplane.'

'And the fledglings?'

'One died, one survived. A human found it, screeching for food, and brought it up. When it was old enough, they set it free in some park.'

'Do you remember the name of the park?' Bram asks, feeling his down feathers stand up in growing alarm.

'Started with an 'M'. Mag-magnet?'

'Magnolia Park?'

'That's it! I wonder where that kid is now. How it's doing. You know, I always felt a bit guilty that I was part of this tragedy, even though I was only doing my job. I always wondered If I could have helped the kid in some way.' His father stops and looks at him. 'What's wrong? Why do you look so shocked?'

Birdie
She has no memories of her parents, although she has seen a few New Caledonian crows at the rescue centre, and has thus formed a vague idea of what her father and mother must have looked like. Through them, and through the many birds that come and go from the centre, she has also learnt what had happened to them, and how she ended up in the hands of a gracious human couple who rescued and healed broken birds. She also learnt about Bertram and his son, how they had prospered while her parents had perished.

After they finally let her go, she set her heart on

vengeance. For months she researched and then trained (at a police academy) till she was ready.

Though cloaked in grief, Bram was just as arrogant as she had imagined. A trait he must have inherited from his father. Did she feel a tinge of guilt when she framed him for Corvus's death? A little.
Did she feel better that she had avenged her parents?
Not really.

The guilt was now overflowing, seeping into her feathers and making her wings heavy. So focused was she on her own pain that she had completely forgotten about Corvus, and what his family must be going through. (It didn't help that she held a deep grudge against the family for harassing her father.)
So focused was she on Bram's incompetence and arrogance that she had let herself become an insensitive, uncaring being.
Flapping her wings as fast as she could, she flew, hoping it wasn't too late.

Polly
Polly hates her job. Hiding in the bushes, she makes human noises to appease a group of insulted ravens. 'Gooood biiiiirds. Niiice. Pretttty birds,' she says, hoping her voice is like the human children who had thrown rocks at the ravens an hour ago, hoping to maintain peace between the humans and the bird-kind.

Sometimes this ruse works and the birds fly away, grumbling about pesky humans under their breathes, but other times it is not enough. And the victims barrage her with incessant complaints. If the humans only killed and consumed birds, it wouldn't have been a huge problem. It was the fact that some of them played so cruelly with birds, clipping their wings, caging them, at times outright torturing them.

There was no respect.

After the ravens fly away, Polly heads over to soothe a goose who wanted to murder a human who had dared to run right past him. The human didn't hit him or tease him, but the goose still took offense. Polly spends two hours trying to control the angry bird.

Then come the ducks, one of whom has eaten too much bread. Followed by a pigeon who is looking for a new place from where she can shit on humans. ('Why have you come to me for this?' Polly asks. 'You are the police?' the pigeon replies. 'I am. But this is not my job,' Polly coolly answers. 'Oh,' says the pigeon, and flies away.) And then one more goose, angry but not sure why.

They all come to her with their problems, even though there are entire teams of birds waiting to help. She can't even say no to them. Mayur is adamant that he shouldn't lose any votes because the 'police were too busy with who and which division should handle a case'.

And then there was *Bram*.

It was an awful thing that happened to him. But she really wished he would do something about it, either seek help or let someone help him. She had thought of assisting him herself, but there had always been some minor grievance or the other that she had ended up getting entangled in at the last minute. She had hoped that Birdie's presence might make him feel lighter, or might make him open up about his feelings …

Mayur is just about to leave Police Grove, having warned Polly that the crows are starting to complain about Bram's behaviour, when Birdie flies up to her and tells her that Bram himself might be a suspect.

'You'd last told me it was a heart attack?' Polly asks her.

'Yes, but it may have been induced,' Birdie says. 'He might hav—'

'Do you have any concrete proof? Or is this all circumstantial?'

'Well, nothing is 100 per cent yet but—'

'Oh, how does that matter!' Mayur jumps in. 'Just use this as an excuse and send him on leave.'

'Yes, but ...' Polly starts.

'It'll do him some good, this time off.' Mayur has already taken a decision.

'And what will we tell the crows?' Polly asks.

'It was a heart attack, wasn't it?' Mayur says as he gracefully flies away.

'I think someone murdered Corvus.'

Polly turns her head to look at Birdie.

'Isn't that why Bram was sent away?' she asks.

'Yes. No. I mean, I think someone truly did kill Corvus. His daughter just came to me with the news that most of his cache at the restaurant is missing.'

'And? Maybe someone took off with the cache after the murder? How does this prove anything?'

'His daughter also said that very few birds knew of the cache's location. Family members, trusted employees, that sort. There was no way anyone else ... no way Bram could have known about it.'

Mayur

The human children stare at him and giggle. Some even try to come close to him, but a human adult snatches the child away just before Mayur could do anything. (He probably wouldn't have done anything, he liked coming to the zoo. And doing something as stupid as harming a human would have barred him for sure, maybe even led to him being killed.)

He leaves the children and their harried parents behind, and starts walking towards his favourite enclosure. He walks past the apes, the elephants, the crocodiles and pauses at the reptilian centre. Involuntarily, a feeling of deep disdain rises up inside him. *How he hates those cold-hearted, wingless rascals.*

He doesn't know when it came to pass, but as far back as he can remember, humans have had their own world and the rest of the animals have had theirs. While the birds, rats, cats and butterflies—the rest—have a basic idea of how human society works, the humans have no idea what goes on in a world where they are not the focal point. Every two years, the non-humans elect someone as the collective head to represent them. It's a cushy job, there isn't really much to do. It's the animal advisors who do the real job. The dogs have a feisty dachshund-corgi mix representing them, the frogs have a wise bull frog for their leader, the squirrels have a hyper Indian palm squirrel. But there are two groups that take his role seriously, and whose population inevitably ends up vying for the mayoral job.

First, there are the birds.

And then there are the reptiles.

Mayur first saw Hisster in a park outside the zoo. He was out there canvassing votes, chatting to potential voters, when the rattlesnake turned up and tried to convince the residents of the park to vote for him instead.

'I know what you're doing,' Mayur had said, fed up after a point.

'What issss it that I'm doing?' Hisster had replied. It was his first mayoral race, while Mayur had already had a stint at the job a few years ago.

'You're trying to steal my votes,' the peacock had replied as calmly as possible.

'Issss this sssstealing? Or issss it jussssst campaigning?'

'Why are you following me?'

'Am I? Aren't we jusssst at the sssssssame park at the sssssssssame time?'

Mayur knew that a snake would be his adversary, but he didn't know who it was going to be. Seeing Hisster out in the open, going after the residents of the park after he'd talked to them, Mayur had realised it wouldn't be as easy as the win against the ageing cobra the first time he had put his name forward for this position.

He had walked up to the sneering snake and lowered his head. 'I better not see you follow me into the next park,' he had whispered.

'What if I do?' The snake seemed unfazed.

Mayur won the election, but that didn't stop Hisster from annoying the peacock. He would turn up in random places, even intimidate Mayur's associates. The snake turned up at the zoo where Mayur lived during the day. Before Mayur could alert the humans though, Hisster quickly escaped the enclosure.

Surely and steadily, the snake was harassing the peacock. But none of it ever crossed the line enough to be classified as a crime. So, technically, there was nothing the peacock could do ... except to enlist the services of Corvus.

He knew the crow was a tough nut, and was capable of much more if given a chance. And for a long time, Corvus did all sorts of odd jobs for him. He stole, he threatened, he fought, he even murdered a few from Hisster's camp. The snake responded in kind.

But then came a time when Corvus wanted out. He got spooked all of a sudden and wanted to retire to a more peaceful life. Mayur let him go then, thinking of enlisting the local assassin, a collared crow, for the job. But by the time he had finally decided to hire the collared crow, the assassin had disappeared. And soon enough Corvus went off too. Mayur had a feeling that the snake had set the very same assassin on Corvus.

Above him, on the tree he's standing under, a group of crows is eyeing him warily. They have been after his life trying to get Bram banished from the police. Something about that raven just rubs them the wrong way.

Even though he has sent the CI away, they are still not satisfied with the outcome. He walks away from them now, can't stand the gaze of so many staring at him woefully.

After a few minutes, Mayur finds himself outside the lion enclosure, looking at the so-called mighty beasts rolling around on the ground. *It's odd*, he thinks, *how humans think of them as being brutal and scary when there are far more vicious animals in the world.*

'Look, mommy! A parrot is flying right towards us,' a little human yells to its parent and Mayur swiftly turns its head to look above.

Polly? What is she doing here?

Nyx and Dargon

'Ma'am, please, this is the third time we've caught you placing your egg in a crow's nest.' Nyx sounds exhausted.

'That egg is your responsibility,' Dargon adds. 'You cannot hand it over to someone else.'

'I have no idea what you're talking about,' Koel the cuckoo says, quite offended.

'So, that's not yours?' Dargon says. They are all standing around a nest with four screaming chicks inside it. One of them looks a bit different.

'Which one?' Koel answers. 'They all look the same to me.'

'One of them has spots,' Nyx says.

'Well, maybe that one just has a lot of personality.' Koel is quite adamant.

'Ma'am, that is your child,' Nyx says.

'I really don't know why you think it's mine. I've never even been on this tree. You two just dragged me here, saying

I had lost something, and then showed me this beautiful baby which, I'd like to say again, is *not mine*.'

Nyx feels tired, Dargon feels like flying into a glass window and hitting his head. They had asked that a separate department handle all cuckoo-related cases, but no one paid any heed. The petty crime detectives from non-corvid trees had also demanded the same, but they too had been ignored. No politician wanted to create a department that would target a particular bird group, thereby alienating potential voters.

Dargon tries another path. He flies down to a branch where Fana, the mother-crow, had been waiting all this while. She had felt like she was being watched for the past ten days, and then noticed Koel (who was now arguing with Nyx above) staring at her from a neighbouring tree, always looking tense and apprehensive. It was only today, when her chicks had hatched, that the cuckoo had flown away to a tree at the other end of the park, looking quite relieved.

All of it had seemed really weird to Fana, so she had asked her partner (who was now out grabbing lunch) to contact Nyx and Dargon. The two detectives, used to cases like these, had instantly recognised that something was amiss in the nest, and had apprehended Koel, the only cuckoo that lived in the park.

'Ma'am,' Dargon says, 'I think it's best that you ask Koel to take her child away.'

'Oh, is she not … listening to you?' asks Fana.

'I think it might be better if you talked to her on your own. Sometimes it helps if things of this … nature are resolved between the two parties.'

'I don't think it was a good idea for them to talk it out,' Nyx says. They are on their way to the police grove.

'Well, the cuckoo wasn't listening to us. What could we have done? There was no proof that the spotted chick was hers, and not some other cuckoo's. If the crow still has a problem, she'll come and file a proper complaint.'

'Yes, but you know how clever they are. She'll probably convince the crow that it's actually good for her to keep the cuckoo's child, that its presence will somehow ward off predators—'

'That's true, though. I've overheard eagles complaining on the Department of Accipitridae tree that a cuckoo fledgeling let out such a bad stink that he had to leave the nest, and look for someone else to eat.'

'When was this?'

'I don't know. Maybe a year ago.'

'And where was I?'

'Don't know.'

'Hmm. Why didn't you tell me about it?'

'Well, I … must have slipped my mind,' he finished.

A minute passes in silence before Nyx asks, 'And why were the eagles complaining about it?'

'I think they said it was unfair, and they were really hungry. I'm not sure if there is an actual law about this—'

'There isn't. Their kind is just really entitled.' They are near the police grove now, and Nyx still can't believe that Dargon had the chance to eavesdrop on a piece of gossip and never shared it with her.

Although they were different kinds of corvids, they had never been a divide amongst them. Their parents had been friends, nesting and roosting on the same trees. And that familiarity had carried on to their children as well. Nyx and Dargon, and their respective partners, were still neighbours in Green Sky Park.

'Are you still upset about the eagles?' Dargon asks as he settles down on his branch.

'Yes,' Nyx simply answers.

'Nyx? Dargon?'

Both of them look up to see Polly with a New Caledonian crow beside her. 'I'm taking her to meet the other departments, but I thought I'd introduce her to you two first. This is Birdie, Bram's new partner.'

'There's something odd about her,' Dargon softly says. 'Don't know if it's good or bad, but there is something definitely ... different about her.'

'Who?' Nyx asks. She looks around.

'Bram's new assistant,' he whispers.

Bram and Birdie are sitting just above them, quiet, lost in thought.

Before Nyx can think of an answer, Ciara the magpie urgently flies over to them. She looks quite upset as she explains how every single nut and seed she had accumulated over the past month, to eat later or to exchange for a piece of meat, has disappeared from where she had stored them.

'Did anyone else know about it? Know where you had kept them?' Nyx asks.

'No, I was quite careful. But ... oh, I don't know. Maybe someone saw me? But it can't be a neighbour. They are all so nice and welcoming.'

'Are you sure about that?' Dargon asks, fidgeting. He can hear Bram and Birdie talking above, but can't pay attention to it. He can feel that they are talking about something important.

'Yes, of course. I mean, I think ...'

'Ma'am,' Nyx says. 'I think we'll need to speak to all of them.'

'Have you seen any suspicious activity in this area? In the past few days?' Nyx asks.

'No,' a treepie who lives above Ciara answers. 'I don't think so. No.'

'And have you seen any strangers around this tree?' Dargon asks.

'There might have been. I'm not sure about that.'
'Hmm,' Dargon says. 'And you live alone?'
'I do. I'm still looking for a mate.'
'So you have no alibi?' Nyx asks.
'Now, look here,' the treepie says. 'There is no need to accuse me of a crime since I'm single at the moment. That's … that's … discrimination.'

Nyx is amused, but doesn't say anything, while Dargon tells the treepie they'll come back to him if they had any questions.

'Do you think he's hiding something?' Dargon whispers to Nyx, as they fly to the treetop.

'No. I think he was just embarrassed he hadn't found a partner yet.'

'You think so?'
'Hmm. And Dargon?'
'Yes?'
'I overheard Birdie talking to Bram earlier. I know what's odd about her.'

'Well then. What is it?'

Nyx doesn't say anything, so Dargon looks at her as they reach the very top.

'Aah,' he says. 'I see. This is payback for the eagles?'
'It is.'
'So you won't tell me?'
'Nope.'

At the top, they notice a newly built nest, but no birds to call it their home. They look around, take their time. A few minutes later, when they are about to leave, a young tufted jay couple arrives at the nest, curious and nervous.

'Is something the matter?' the male asks.
'You left the nest all alone?' Nyx enquires.
'Yes, well,' he puffs up his feathers. 'We were getting a few more twigs for the nest.'

'Where are they?' Nyx asks, noticing their empty claws. 'The twigs?'

'Oh,' the female speaks up. 'We ... couldn't find the ... right kind.'

'I see,' says Nyx.

'Yes, we are expecting, you see. So, the nest is for ...' says the male.

'... the eggs,' finishes the female.

'Yes, that's what usually happens,' Dargon comments. 'The parents make a nest for the eggs.'

'Why does it seem like you two are hiding something?' Nyx asks, slightly bored.

'Us? No, of course not,' the male says, feathers shivering.

'We're just nervous—first-time parents, you know?' the female adds.

'Sure,' Dargon says, playing along. 'We are actually here because of a robbery. Know anything about it?'

'No, we don't know. How horrible. Who has been robbed? Are you allowed to tell us?' the female says.

'Ciara, who lives—'

'Oh yes, we met her. She seems like a lovely magpie,' says the female.

'Awful to think this happened to her,' adds the male.

'Hmm. And do you have any idea who could have done this?' asks Nyx. 'Seen anyone strange near this tree lately?'

'Strange? No, don't think so.' The male looks at the female.

'Anyone new?' Dargon asks.

'New?' The male gives an involuntary hop.

Dargon and Nyx exchange a look. They have never met a corvid as nervous as this one, so incapable of hiding his secrets.

'Ma'am,' Dargon tries a different route. 'I really think you should tell us what's wrong. What are you not telling us?'

Corvus

Corvus bars the restaurant's cardboard flap with a nifty twig and takes flight. He feels like singing, although he doesn't have the voice for it. He lets out a few (what he thinks are) musical caws.

He can't help it. Business is booming. Both the front and the side ones. His family is safe and secure. And though sometimes an anonymous bird comes to attack him from the skies, it doesn't do much more than bump into him. It's annoying for sure, but not threatening.

Of course, if ever he manages to catch the bird, he'll rip it to shreds.

Six months ago, he was in a different state of mind. Corvus had barged into Mayur's office, flustered but determined, and told him he won't do any of that shady business anymore. 'But if you need me to do other sorta work … sure, I'll do that,' he finished.

Mayur had no expression on his face as he stared at Corvus. 'What do you mean by "shady business"? And what exactly do you mean by "other sorta work"?'

'It's simple, Boss. I don't wanna kill anymore. The more I kill, the more someone wants to kill *me*. See, they don't care that you ordered the hit, they only see who—'

'Got it. You don't want to assassinate anyone.'

'Yes, but I can still steal or … or … intimidate someone, you know? There's no real danger in that.'

'I see.'

'So that's okay with you, Boss?'

The peacock gave him a hard glare. 'You've caught me at a bad time, Corvus. If it were any other day, I would have pecked your eyes out. But there is a lot of treachery afoot today, and I've got to take care of some … business. You've been direct with your issues and I appreciate that.'

'Thank you, Boss. I will do anyth—'

'Leave. Now.'
'Of course, absolutely,' Corvus said as he took off.

Corvus had always known when to start a new venture and when to end it. There was a delicate balance when it came to business, as with anything in life. And he had an innate sense of getting out of the game before disaster struck.

And even better sense to find good allies.

He made a deal with the cats to ensure they wouldn't trouble his customers. (He had to give them two carcasses a day.) And he made a deal with Mayur—right after his family's tree was lost a year ago. He helped the politician, who in turn helped him (get three lovely birch trees in Oak Shadow Park, a restaurant space he didn't have to pay rent for and many more things).

It was all a matter of balance. Delicate balance. Who to befriend, who not to. Who to keep at bay as your enemy. Where to live, where to kill those who came in the way. What to eat, what to store away.

Corvus had used every one of his learnings to amass a huge cache of nuts and seeds, which he kept hidden near his restaurant and replenished from time to time with fresh nuts and seeds. The ones on the verge of rot were eaten by members of his family, or were given away as salary to his employees.

Sure, sometimes they complained that they wouldn't be able to store them for long as cache. But he told them they could either stay with him or leave. He said the same to birds like Domino, who grew too big for their boots. Asking for a raise! A raise! For what? Ferrying a piece of meat to a customer? He had shoved that nutcracker right out of the restaurant then.

Corvus always tells everyone he is a decent bird. He doesn't want to fight, he really doesn't. But there are times when fate forces him to act. And he does.

For example, one day he saw a collared crow, no, *the* collared crow at his restaurant and was just filled with rage. All he could speak out was 'You!' as he pushed him out. The nerve of that bird! To step into his establishment a month after he ...

He shakes his head as he approaches his home-park. Corvus feels rage fill up inside him, and he drops down to the ground. He needs to cool down, he needs to find a couple of ants.

Corvus had first taken up anting when he and his entire family were evicted because of that idiot of a New Caledonian. The stress was too much back then, and all he wanted to do was kill that landlord. Peck him to death. But after days of rubbing ants on his wings, he had calmed down and had decided to get into a few businesses—the restaurant one, and then politics—to create stability for his family.

When Mayur had first stood for elections as the city's All Animal Mayor, Corvid had instantly realised he had to approach Mayur and offer his services to him. And from thereon he (and a few of his restaurant employees) had stolen, fought and killed for the peacock.

Until one day, as he was flying close to a few electric cables, he had found himself being pushed into them. He'd turned around just in time to see a collared crow—*the* collared crow—flying away. He was quite famous. A mercenary who worked for everyone. Who loved to shove animals into wires and electrocute them.

The snake must have sent him. Although he didn't get the time to think that back then. It was only when he woke up later at a human's rescue centre for birds that he pieced together what had happened to him.

He was grateful for the human's help, rare as it was to see them do something so kind and unselfish. But was quite annoyed by the incessant questions of the rescue centre orphans who had never lived outside the human's home.

One young New Caledonian, in particular, just wouldn't stop with her queries about where he lived and who all lived there.

He was glad to leave that place.

Corvus is finished with the anting. He feels much, *much* better now. Just as he is just about to take off, he stumbles. 'Who the—' He turns around to accost whoever had bumped into him.

'You!' he says, just before he dies.

Merle
It's night at Oak Shadow Park. The humans usually keep the lights on even at such a late hour, nearly midnight, but the power is out within a five-kilometre radius. There is rain and thunder all around, and the sight of the sudden lighting is the only thing guiding Merle towards the dead tree she calls her office.

It's difficult going, she feels cold and heavy. The water has drenched her feathers, made the ground underneath her muddy and soft. But still she is holding on to the left wing of the dead sparrow, gripping it tight with her beak. She was lucky she found the unidentified body in the park itself, and not have to go to the graveyard and come across *them* again.

She shivers in fear, drags the dead bird to the base of her office, and then inside the hollow. Now, at last, she can begin her examination in earnest.

Ever since she became the corvid-doctor, she began to be called upon to investigate all sorts of ailments, things she could only guess at, based on complaints and outward examinations. But Merle didn't believe in just theories and words, she wanted to dig inside and actually get her beak dirty. It was not enough for her to know that all birds have a heart, lung and gizzard. Merle wanted to see all the organs for herself. She wanted to know how they function. How could she treat anyone with clarity if she didn't know what was going on inside?

She couldn't rely on the small bird carcasses she consumed from Corvus's restaurant once in a while. They were in ruins, half eaten, imperfect. Roadkills were worse. Flattened and crushed.

It was with this intention that she first flew to the avian graveyard in search of a corvid subject, but came across a group of feral felines instead. They taunted her, the five tabby cats, and hissed at her to stay away from their territory.

'If you come here again,' the leader, a queen who only had one eye, said, 'we will dismember you and gobble you up within seconds.'

She was flying above them then, way out of their reach, but she still felt scared and helpless, unable to think of a retort in that moment. That night, when she returned to her hollow, shaken and disturbed, Merle forgot all about her quest for science. All she could think about was a way to get back at the cats.

If only she was a bigger bird, unafraid of death …

As another round of thunder booms across the park, Merle sets to work and opens up the sparrow lying feet up inside the hollow. With her beak, she carefully splits open the underside and picks out the organs within. She throws the stomach and liver out—resolving to eat them later so as to not waste them—and hops over to the rat she had killed earlier in the day. It's already cut open, making it easier for her to cut through the vessels and gently take out its heart.

Merle takes it to the sparrow and fits it inside, next to the bird's own heart. She steps outside for second, to tear a clump of grass from the earth, and is back inside once again, ready to tie up the two hearts.

It doesn't work the first time.

The conditions are right. When Merle sets the sparrow outside, hoping for a hit of lightning, it strikes the bird right in the heart only a few minutes later. The dead bird jumps in the air, thuds to the ground and bounces on the mud a few times. Then, in jerky movements, it flaps its wings and tries to fly but falls down every time.

Merle is not disappointed. This was only a trial run. She wanted to see if it was possible, and now she knew that it *was*.

She waits weeks till she gets lucky again. This time, she finds a collared crow electrocuted by a few cable wires near a human's house. It shocks her, but also gives her an idea. No other bird is around at that moment. Merle herself was there by chance, having heard that the house had recently been occupied by a family of rats. She had heard a hiss when she arrived, and did not know whether it was a cat or a snake. Not that she looked forward to meeting either kind. So, she had waited in a tree till it was all clear.

And then she had heard it: a scuffle, a surprised caw and the thud of a dead crow landing on a pile of leaves.

As quickly as possible, Merle dragged the crow into the Oak Shadow Park and into her hollowed tree. She is careful, but is really lucky not to have come across another bird. Merle doesn't want anyone to think she kills and eats her own kind. There are some that do when the situation is dire. But there is no just cause to become a cannibal in a plentiful park.

She has an inkling of how the human world works, and though there is no rain in the sky and no thunder and lightning to go with it, Merle gets on with her work and cuts open another rat, picks out another heart to safely stitch inside the dead bird's cavity. She knows a place where wires and cables protrude from a lamppost in a secluded area of the park. She knows she must take this crow there, to restart the hearts.

Her ties of grass are strong, and she is sure that the crow will have a better chance at being alive again. Corvids are stronger, bigger, more intelligent. There is no doubt in her head that this experiment will work.

At first, Merle only lets out the reanimated crow at the dead of night, so it could fly around and get used to the surroundings. When she thought the crow had roamed enough, she would let out a stern 'return to me', and the crow would come back to her. Slowly, she increased the range, and soon enough the once-dead crow was flying within a three-kilometre radius of the park.

'Tonight we will visit the quarrelsome cats,' Merle told it one night, finally. 'We will show them that birds are mightier, and far more intelligent than them. Years of living with humans, and around them, has weakened their spirit. We will show them, won't we?'

The reanimated crow let out a scratchy 'yes, mistress' in response, and together they stepped out of the hollow and took to the night sky.

They flew over trees and houses, streets and alleys alike to reach the garbage dump. As soon as they landed among the trash, two tabby cats came out of their hiding places and began to hiss at them both.

'Back again, crow?' one of the felines asked.

'Do you wish to die?' another asked.

'No. No,' Merle answered, casually hopping closer to the cats. 'I wanted to introduce you to a friend of mine,' she said, turning her head to look at the once-dead corvid, letting out a single 'attack!'

'Yes, mistress,' came the reply.

As they flew back to Oak Shadow Park, they could still hear the cats wailing, crying as they tried to come to terms with the scratches inflicted upon them. This was only a warning, next time Merle would have to be better prepared—perhaps she would need another ... soldier.

'Who is that, mistress?'

Merle looked at the collared crow, and then down below. 'Oh, him?' she asked, spotting Corvus leaving his restaurant. 'That's Corvus. Did you know him ... before?'

'Don't know, mistress. But I feel angry for some reason.'

'Hmm. I wouldn't be surprised if he picked fights with you when you were ... alive.'

The moment she said that, the collared crow flew down and bumped into Corvus, disorienting him and causing him to stumble. It was so sudden that the restaurateur could not see who had attacked him, and could not take off after the once-dead crow.

'Why did you do that?' Merle asked when it came back up.

'I don't know, mistress.'

'Hmm.'

'Mistress?'

'Yes?'

'What is my name?'

She named it Frankie. She had never met an undead bird before, and didn't know if it was a quality shared by all of them, but she did find this one at least to be quite frank and honest. *Frankie*.

A day after she told it its name, Frankie came up to her and asked her for another favour.

'You are lonely?' Merle repeated its words.

'Yes, mistress.'

'But I don't understand—'

'You go home after work, mistress, to your partner and children. But I have to stay here, inside the hollow, or roam the skies above, all alone. I don't even remember if I had a family ... before, but I think ... I feel that I must have.

Otherwise, why do I long for some sort of partnership? Why do I feel so, so sad when no one is here?'

'I don't know what to say.'

'Will you find someone for me, mistress?'

'I can't promise. I mean ... it was by chance that I found you! I can't be sure that—'

'Please, mistress? Please, could you try?'

The next day, as she was flying from her roost at Green Sky Park to her office in Oak Shadow Park, a dwarf jay that was flapping his wings next to her suddenly stopped moving and dropped dead to the ground.

Oldrick

Oldrick is fifteen years old, older than most birds that live in Elm Grove Park. He has a year left in him at most. And he's made peace with it.

He looks at Bram stumbling around the park, anting up and breaking down. He is so full of despair that Oldrick doesn't know if he should interfere or just let the raven process his emotions on his own.

Still unsure, he flies down from his roost. The other birds in the park are choosing to ignore the Corvid Inspector, as they have the past few nights Bram has returned to his former home. A few that tried to talk some sense into him have faced an angry raven, irritated and imbalanced, in need of a scuffle to ease his pain.

Oldrick is calm as he settles on the grass nearby. Bram is in a haze, but he still tries to walk up to the old jay, who tentatively asks if he is okay.

'What?' Bram tries to say, but stumbles with his words too. Oldrick feels even more sad for him.

It was that time of the day when everyone was out looking for food. Oldrick had already eaten, the boon of being an early riser. He was already on his tree, enjoying the quietude of a morning when human sounds were at a minimum.

He closed his eyes.

He opened them again as a screech filled the air and a hooting mass of feathers and speed-wooshed over his tree, heading for a young raven couple's nest. His warning call came a bit too late, frozen as he was in place. Not quite comprehending what had happened while it was happening.

Oldrick did his duty and informed the police, but he could never tell Bram what he had seen that day. The owls had intended to eat the eggs, but had heard Oldrick's call and disappeared.

There is an old woman whose garden he visits sometimes. He does it more for her than for himself. He knows she would worry if he didn't visit her once in a while, sit at her feet, hover near her head, eat seeds and nuts from her offered hand.

She used to have a husband. He was just as sweet as her. But he had a terrible, terrible end. An unsure step, and then a cracked head on the pavement outside their home. He'd wanted to check on an exposed wire that had killed a few birds.

Oldrick had seen it all unfold—early as he was for his visit.

A few days ago, he was on his way to the garbage dump when he saw an unmoving clump of black on the ground. He swooped down to investigate, already wondering if he knew the bird. At closer range, he quickly recognised the body as belonging to the restaurateur or mob boss, depending on whom he was talking to.

It was a sorry sight. His eyes as black as a starless sky.

He doesn't know if humans know more about death. They do seem just as scared of it as the birds. And when one of them leaves, he sees the grief that spreads though their wingless bodies.

Is it fear and sadness brought on by knowledge? Do they know about the starless sky? Do they know what it feels like?

Or are they just as clueless as the birds? Is it a fear born of the unknown?

Oldrick isn't afraid. His life has been long, and he has seen as much of the world as he had wanted to. He is gifted with contentment—happy where he is, where he will inevitably die. If he had been someone *more*, someone who had wanted more from life, he might have had been plagued with regrets and unfulfilled desires.

He might have wanted to live somewhere else. Or fly over to the forest nearby. He might have found someone else after his partner's death. Eaten more nuts, buried more seeds. Might have told Bram what he saw that day. Or fought the owls himself. He might have flown so high that he could touch the stars, and flown down to the old dying man and kept him company in his dying moments. He might have kept in touch with all of his children.

But he is Oldrick, someone who is enough. He doesn't let his mind rest on these thoughts too long.

Domino
He's always been an ambitious nutcracker, always wanted more from life. As a chick he wanted more food, as a fledgling he wanted to fly higher, and as an adult all he ever wanted was *more cache*.

He started out working hard, trying the straight road, but all he found were barriers. Every time he came close to the good life, someone clipped his wings and pushed him out of the nest. And then he had to rebuild again. It was only when he met Corvus that he realised he had to *take* what was owed to him, not lie in wait for someone to give it to him. The crow taught him to lie and cheat, kill and maim, press against a wound and demand his due.

I'm so very close, Domino thinks, as he spots a magpie burying her cache near the nest he is working on, *to getting all that I deserve.*

Ciara
It's always a shock to other birds to hear that Ciara provides funerary services.

'But you look so happy!'
'You are so ... normal?'
'Have you ever felt like ... eating them?'
'Aren't you creeped out?'
She answers all questions with a smile:
'Thank you?'
'If you say so!'
'No.'
'Not really.'

And truly, she doesn't think there's anything wrong with what she does. She believes her role as the mediator between life and death—between the relatives who mourn for their dead ones and the humans (usually the gardeners) she directs towards the dead birds—is a crucial one. If she wasn't there to play out her responsibilities, the dead bird would just lie there in front of everyone, slowly degrading over time. And perhaps even get eaten (by a cat, usually) in front of everyone.

She ensures that the dead are carefully taken away to hidden posts—garbage bins, trucks or dumps—so that the eating and degradation too is hidden.

Ciara ferries the dead, but she also consoles the living. She says a few words over the recently departed, allows the families to pour out their grief and, on one occasion, stood still and silent as the Corvid Inspector picked a fight with Corvus's brother and daughter.

She settles down on her tree, on her branch, ready to rest for some time. But her stomach calls out for a feeding. Hers is a lovely spot in Walnut Season Park. Not many humans come around to this corner, leaving the residents in relative peace.

Ciara absolutely loves the place.

But.

She feels lonely too.

Surrounded all over by mated pairs and squeaking chicks, she wishes she had someone to build a nest with as well. And it's not like they have to build it themselves, there are plenty of couples who outsource the building of their nest—let professionals do a safer and better job. A young pair up-branch have contracted a builder too, last she heard. She has enough gathered in her cache to pay for it all ...

... which reminds her.

Ciara, still thinking of nests and fledglings, flies down to the ground in search of the spot where she had buried her cache, a mix of nuts and seeds she had decided to use only for monetary purposes. (Although, truth be told, she ate some of it too when she felt particularly lazy about going to hunt for food.)

She lands with grace, hops over to the cache and digs with her bill. First this way and then that. But no matter what, she doesn't find anything. Growing more frustrated by the minute, she digs up the surrounding area too, until at last she has dug up forty holes around her.

Tired and helpless, she feels hatever anger there was in her dissipate. Still, a spark ignites in her brain, and she remembers that there are those who can help her solve this problem.

From below, she looks up at the tree where she resides. Dargon and Nyx left four hours ago, having questioned her neighbours. They left in quite a hurry, and refused to tell her if they had a suspect. She doesn't know if one of her neighbours stole her cache or if it was someone else.

It seems absurd to even think that any of the other residents would rob her. But then again, she did have a trusting nature. When her partner had left her for another bird, he had not once given her a sign that he was planning on leaving.

Would she have to leave this tree?

She has just taken off from the tree when she crashes into another magpie. They fall to the ground, having lost their balance. But thankfully there's a pile of leaves beneath them and into it they fall.

'I'm so sorry,' they both say at the same time, finding their wings entangled with each other's.

'That's fine,' they both answer at the same time.

'You're a magpie too?' Ciara asks him once they have separated. It's a dumb question, and Ciara realises that the moment her beak closes.

But the other magpie laughs. 'I am. My name is Kieran, and I'm actually moving into this tree today.'

'You are? I didn't know I—'

'I'll be taking up on a branch at the fifth level.'

'Oh, I live there!'

'Well, what a coincidence!'

Ciara feels all the more embarrassed now at having bumped into her new neighbour.

But he saves her from that feeling of uneasiness. 'This day has been an interesting one for me. Before I, um, met you, I saw a rook and a jackdaw chasing a nutcracker in the skies. A crow and raven also joined the two in the chase.'

'What?'

'Yeah, and the nutcracker seemed to be way ahead of them too. And would have probably escaped into the woods nearby if a pair of dwarf jay and collared crow hadn't come out of nowhere and just crashed into the nutcracker. They had this *unusual* energy about them. They flew like birds, but they also didn't seem like real birds ... For a moment I thought maybe the humans had built something to look like us? But I don't know. I don't know what to think.'

At the back of her mind, Ciara is aware that Dargon and Nyx will soon come to visit her. But she is busy right now talking to Kieran, and can't make herself think of anything but the future. They are on the fifth level of the tree, sitting on Ciara's branch at the moment.

'So,' she starts, raking up courage, 'is your partner also coming to this tree?'

'Oh no. I'm single. Quite single. And ... are there any other magpies in this tree?

'No. No. Just the two of us,' she says.

He laughs. 'Two for joy!'

Epilogue
Bram still can't decide if he should go back. There was nothing there for him. Here, near his father, away from humans and their loud noises, their cruelty, he could live in peace. Maybe one day, he could think of starting a family again.

That thought was his father's suggestion. He agreed that his son needed to heal first and take some time to do so, but he also didn't want Bram to give up at such a young age. To make Bram understand his point better, he also brought in a neighbour of his to visit Bram one day.

'Verona?' Bram says. He is on his father's roosting branch, looking nowhere in particular, thinking about his life and the choices he has made. He is quite surprised to see his old senior, the former Corvid Inspector, land on the opposite branch with his father flapping his wings behind her.

'You never told me *she* lived here!' he asks incredulously as the other two caw with laughter.

'I did tell you I was moving to the woods,' Verona says.

'Yes,' he answers. 'But I didn't think ... wait, are *you* the friend who told Dad about Corvus being nearly killed? How did you know? Why didn't you tell me?'

'It was all hush-hush,' she answers. 'Mayur wanted it investigated. Corvus was on Mayur's payrolls, you know. He left right after the electrocution.'

'Oh.' Bram had heard rumours of Corvus working for Mayur, but he didn't think it was true.

Verona notices his thoughtful expression and crooks her head to the side. 'How have you been, Bram? I heard about ... you know. It can't have been easy.'

'It wasn't. It isn't.'

'You are still grieving, I can see. And your father told me you are thinking of leaving the police force?'

Bram looks at Bertram, wondering what else he has told this former senior. But his father stands still, he wants Verona to do the talking, it seems.

'Well, they don't want me there—' Bram begins.

Verona jumps in: 'Your father explained the circumstances to me. You are one of the brightest ravens I have ever met. Grief has made your mind foggy, it's made you despondent. You too have seen that in the victims' families and grieving families. Haven't you? It's quite difficult when it happens to you, of course.'

'What do you think I should do then? I don't see the point in anything if someone can just come and destroy everything in a second. A fellow bird, the humans ... they killed my family.'

Verona hops closer. Her voice is soft as she says, 'We steal eggs, kill rodents and eat them. We eat all sorts of dead things. We do not care when we are the predators, but when it's the other way around, when a human kills one of us, sometimes maims us for play, we suddenly realise how truly violent the world is.'

Bram feels overwhelmed. He can't think of a proper response. But his senior isn't finished. Her voice even softer, she says, 'Then again, there are humans who feed us, fellow birds who keep us company when we roost, berries and nuts so juicy and filling and the sky ... the sky so blue and wide. Even if it rains and the sky gets grey and dark and we must hide and stay clear of it, even if we fear our roosting tree might fall, we do not give up. Deep down, we know that nothing bad lasts forever.'

'Nothing good lasts either,' Bram counters.

'Yes, Bram. That is why your job is so important, why *you* are so important. You are the sun that drives away the stormy clouds, the strong tree that provides shelter, you are the one that rights the wrongs.'

Bram has made up his mind, Bertram can see that quite clearly. But it seems his son hasn't quite accepted his own decision. He needs a push, only a little push, and he will do the right thing, once again.

SWOOOOSH!

An unknown bird lands on his tree, and hops over straight to Bram whose face grows angrier by the second.

'What are *you* doing here?' he asks.

'I'm so sorry, Bram,' the bird answers. 'I shouldn't have... I was angry, for a long time. I didn't think. I let revenge colour my actions.'

Bertram finally registers that the bird is a New Caledonian. *Oh, this must be Birdie.* For the second time that day, Bertram stands in the background and lets the conversation flow without him.

'I know why you framed me. And why you killed Corvus. You blame us for what happened to your parents and—'

'No, that's not right,' she says, looking nervous but excited. 'I mean, yes, I did frame you, but I didn't kill Corvus.'

'You didn't kill him?' Bram asks, dumbfounded.

'I didn't. And Corvus's daughter told us a few hours ago that the restaurant's cache is missing. I was so hung up on ruining your life that I never helped with the questioning, I never allowed you to question all parties. Maybe we missed someone. Maybe—'

Bram closes his eyes and drives her words away. He flaps his wings as he thinks hard, surprising Bertram and Birdie a bit. He goes over every interrogation in his head. And then suddenly opens his eyes.

'We were so stupid!' he says. 'I was so clouded by grief, you so caught up in your revenge, that we missed the simplest of things.'

'What are you saying?'

'The nutcracker! We never checked his alibi!'

Birdie lets out a caw of surprise. 'You're right!'

Bram doesn't waste any more time. 'We must leave!' he says, already in the air. 'Now!'

Bertram looks up as they leave without acknowledging him, as they furiously fly against the noon-time sky. He is glad to see Bram back again, and relieved to see that Birdie really did grow up right—and was capable of righting her wrongs.

One of these days, he'll ask for her forgiveness.

Crown Shyness

Her ship is all of a sudden moving so fast that she can't comprehend where it is headed. Her mind is foggy, and she is floating in and out of consciousness. She had a destination. Some sort of mission. But she can't recall it now. All she registers is glimpses of green down below.

Until, quite suddenly, her sight goes black.

When she wakes up, still strapped to the seat, she finds herself stuck in a tree, hanging by a deflated parachute (which had sprung from under her seat).

CLICK

She pushes open the seat belt and jumps to the ground, thankful that the drop is only a foot. She looks around, not that surprised she can breathe so easily here. After all, she is surrounded by massive trees all around. They feel overwhelming, more so since she can't see the sky above, only patches of it through the crown-shy trees that have created gaps among their canopies.

She checks her watch and turns the dial in the hope of getting a signal. All she hears is static. 'Not get messages here you.'

She spins around in alarm, searching for the source of the advice.

'I here. Above. Look! Tree!'

She looks, and there he is, a young boy of fourteen or

fifteen, dressed in a dark green leotard.

'You know English?' she asks.

The boy nods. 'It one of dead language. We learn school.' He swings down the branches elegantly, landing with a soft thud in front of her.

Up close she can see the differences between them. Though they are both humans, there is fine, green hair growing on the boy's skin. Sprouting from behind his ears are dark green vines that merge with his medium-length hair. She, on the other hand, appears most like the people that used to live in the BEFORE TIME, when the entire human population was concentrated on Earth.

'Follow me you?' the boy asks, after having studied her just as she had studied him.

Every hut, made entirely of metallic sheets, is set on the forest floor. But every man, woman and child is in the trees, staring at her from the branches. All of them, like the boy, are in leotards.

'She fall down?' a woman about her own age asks the boy. She is right above them, swinging her legs casually.

The boy nods. 'Found her and big balloon.'

Later, the woman tells her about their society. How they were all descendants of the humans who stayed back to help the Earth heal in the aftermath of the catastrophic climate events. In return, the planet protected them.

'You see trees? Everywhere!' the woman says. The two of them are sitting inside a hut.

'I do see trees everywhere, yes.'

'They protect.'

'Sure, we have trees in the biosphere. There are actually twenty parks in there—'

'No. Not same,' the woman says, exasperated, taking hold of her guest's ears and flicking them.

'Oww. What was that for?'

'Oh,' the woman says, realising that the guest's ears are different.

'Apology. Please? We *hear* with ears. Everything in forest. Don't need to speak. Can hear what here,' she points at her head. 'Was checking if you ... same ears?'

'No. I don't have the same ears.'

'Hmm. How to tell? What trees are? Oh!' she says. 'Come outside. Come!'

They walk away from the settlement, deep into the woods. On the way, they come across her parachute—in the process of being pulled down by the boy and his friends. He waves a quick hello and goodbye to her as they pass by each other.

'Where are you taking me?' she asks the woman.

'Oh. You see, you believe it.' Through the lush forest they move. There are plants and shrubs, ivy and trees, animals great and small in their path. She can already smell it, the jet fuel of her crashed ship. She expects to come across a mangled aircraft stuck in a massive tree, or a metallic mess on the forest floor. But what she sees makes her wish for the cold, unknown embrace of deep space instead.

For what does one do when one sees giant trees twisting and compressing a huge spaceship with the utmost ease? Crushing it like a tiny bug, squashing the insides and only leaving a thin metal strip as the evidence for its existence.

'You lucky,' the woman beside her says. So cool, composed despite the scene in front of them. 'You have good heart. Trees sense. Trees know. They save you.'

'And what about others who come through? Who maybe don't have a ... good heart?'

The woman grins and claps her hands with glee. 'Like so.'

A few months later, she is still not used to swinging from branch to branch. She is finally used to the leotards though. The treeple, that's what they call themselves, told her that it was the best clothing for moving around. It was flexible, made from the rubbery extract of a sacred tree. And though she now knows what happened to the ones that had been sent before her, and has seen with her own eyes what happened to the ones who were sent after her—her shiny new hut was born out of that—she is still not quite sure why she was spared.

As she lands on the ground with a much louder thud than the others, she looks up and thinks of that very first day. How she had looked up into the patches of blue sky and felt uneasy.

That feeling still remains. Though she is happy to have found refuge, to have finally settled down on land, she can't help but feel like a bird that has been caged inside a pretty enclosure. And that she will never truly be free.

Moss

Day 1

The young couple stands back and admires the small but impressive moss frame they've just nailed to the wall above their dining table.

Jai Prakash looks at Nandini. 'What do you think?'

She drops her gaze to the white cat currently grooming himself on top of the table. 'Do you think it's out of Shallot's reach?'

'Oh, definitely,' Jai Prakash replies. 'I measured both the cat and the distance between the table and the frame.'

'Hmm.'

'I'm positive,' he adds, grinning, stretching out the 'pos' to make it sound like 'paws'.

Nandini snorts. 'I'll still tell him to be careful,' she says, picking Shallots up. 'Don't hurt the moss, okay?' she tells him, staring into his eyes. 'It's your friend.'

'Me-aow,' the cat promises.

Jai Prakash softly pats Shallots on the head, utters a 'good boy' and heads to the kitchen to make breakfast. Nandini, meanwhile, having placed the cat back on the table, clicks a picture of the moss frame and sends it to her family and friends. 'I searched online for moss frames and this one website had really great reviews … so I bought this from there,' she captions it.

'I love it!' one friend says.

'This is so cool,' says another.

Nandini hearts their replies just as her father's message pings: 'Too green,' he states, and then adds, 'How will you water it?'

'I don't need to,' Nandini tells him. 'This moss is dry. It won't grow. It's just for decoration.'

'Okay, good,' he replies.

'Looks so beautiful,' her mother writes in at about the same time, with a collection of her favoured emoticons.

Nandini also sends the picture and caption to the petsitter, a college kid who looks after Shallots when they are away on holidays.

'Haha Shallots is gonna eat it,' comes the comment, followed by, 'But it looks nice.'

Happy that everyone (mostly) liked it, Nandini places the phone on the table and goes to the kitchen to help Jai Prakash with the breakfast.

Day 2

The next morning, when the two walk into the dining room, all bleary-eyed, they catch the cat sitting on the table and staring at the moss frame. Nandini quickly picks him up and asks him what's wrong.

'Ma-ooo-w,' he whimpers.

'Should we take him to the vet?' she asks her husband.

'No,' he says. 'I think he's just scared of the moss.'

'Why would he be scared of the moss?'

He shrugs. 'Cats are weird.'

Day 5

This afternoon, they are in a rush to clean their house. A few friends are coming over for lunch, and it's their first time hosting at the new flat. The tablecloth is new, as is the cover on the sofa. All the plants are freshly watered and the floor is as clean as it can be.

'Should we check where they are? What if they are already here?' Nandini asks.

'We would have received a call from the guards at the main gate,' Jai Prakash answers.

'Hmm,' Nandini says.

'I'll check with them, see where they are,' Jai Prakash adds.

'Ten minutes away,' comes the reply in the group chat. Their three friends—Shailesh, Rima and Arjun—are sharing a taxi, and they can clearly see the time of arrival on the app.

When they get out, the three scramble for some change among themselves, before realising one of them can just pay the fare through an e-wallet. After they inform the security guard at the gate that they are visiting their friends at 201B, and the guards confirm their visit with a quick call to the couple, they take the lift to the second floor.

'Wow,' Shailesh says. He's the first to enter the house, the first to see how well Jai Prakash and Nandini have decorated their new home. 'This is amazing!'

'I especially love the moss frame,' Rima says. She is right behind Shailesh.

'I agree ... with everything these two just said,' Arjun pipes up, closing the door behind him.

Nandini and Jai Prakash beam as they tell their friends more about the flat, giving them a tour of the place.

Shallots, who has received scritches on his forehead from all three guests, stays back. He spots three glasses of water on the table and decides to investigate. He uses his back legs as springs and carves a path through the air to land softly on the table. With purpose, he walks towards the glasses, sniffs at them, nudges them with his nose, before tentatively touching one with his front left paw.

The glass of water doesn't move, so he uses more force, curious to see what might happen next, until at last the glass loses its balance, sways to one side and topples over. A thud, and then water reaches Shallots's paws, making him jump, all four paws in the air. He quickly takes off from the table and lands on the ground, away from the scene of crime. From the floor, he keeps an eyes on the table to see if any water drips off it, as he licks his paws one by one.

Suddenly he stops, tongue mid-lick, as he watches a slow creeping arm of the moss draw closer and closer to the table, till it finds the water and slurps it up.

When Nandini and Jai Prakash return to the room, they are surprised to see Shallots hissing at the dining table from the floor.

'Are you okay?' Nandini asks, picking the cat up.

'Strange,' Jai Prakash says, as he hands out the glasses of water to Rima and Arjun. 'I'm sure I filled the third glass as well ... and it wasn't lying on the side like this when—' He stops, narrows his eyes at the cat. 'Shallots?' he asks, walking closer to the terrified cat in his wife's arms as his guests look on in amusement. 'Did you have something to do with this?'

Day 183
'Umm,' Rima says. She has arrived at short notice. 'Too bored at home,' she had messaged Nandini half an hour before arriving. 'Can I come over?'

Now, as she steps inside the flat, she finds herself unable to say anything as she stares at the wall behind the dining table.

It's covered entirely in moss.

'How did that ...?' she starts, and then pauses. 'I mean, it looks nice, but maybe—' She stops, looks at the anxious faces of Nandini and Jai Prakash. 'An entire wall?' she asks.

'Well ...,' Jai Prakash says.

'... it just kind of happened,' Nandini finishes.

'One day,' Jai Prakash continues, 'I sprayed some water on it and its colour visibly became brighter, so I continued to water it.'

'Then it started to grow ... and before we realised it, the entire wall was green,' Nandini says.

'Oh,' Rima says, noticing Shallots rubbing his sides against the moss. 'It looks ... it looks very lively in here now. Yes, very lively.'

'And Shallots absolutely loves the moss. He was a bit scared of it at first, but now he can't stop scratching himself against that wall,' Nandini says.

Rima's phone vibrates, and she answers a call from a telemarketer. 'Oh no,' she replies, as the call centre employee offers a loan from a bank she's never heard of. 'Do I have to come home? It's that urgent?'

She turns around and walks towards the main door, mouthing a 'sorry' and a 'I'll call you back' to her friends before leaving. Her phone is still stuck to her ear although the telemarketer has disconnected the call. But Rima doesn't care. She needed an excuse to leave. There was a malevolent energy inside their flat, and she needed to *leave*.

Day 251
'So?' Arjun asks. He is sitting in the balcony of Nandini and Jai Prakash's flat, facing the couple in question. Rima and Shailesh are sitting on either side. Shallots is inside, playing with the moss that now covers each and every wall of the living and dining area. A bushy arm protrudes from one wall. It is holding a red ribbon and swaying it from side to side, just out of Shallots's reach.

Rima had messaged Arjun and Shailesh about her last visit, and how she'd left when she'd seen the creepy moss. She'd felt uncomfortable for days afterwards, and the two men had been spooked as well. But that uneasiness had slowly turned to guilt and sadness when they'd realised they were avoiding Nandini and Jai Prakash without ever checking on them.

Still, they didn't know how to approach the subject

without feeling awkward. They found the courage to do so only when, a few days ago, Jai Prakash started posting pictures of the couple on holiday, where they looked so happy, healthy and refreshed.

After a tentative 'hi' from Rima, all three ended up inviting themselves to the couple's home again.

And now they were sitting in the balcony.

'In the beginning,' Nandini says, 'we were quite scared. It just ... started to grow. It took over the wall and we had no idea what to do.'

'When we tried to remove the original frame, it caught hold of our hands and twisted them,' Jai Prakash says.

The three guests look on in horror, and wonder if they should quickly leave, when Nandini laughs and waves a hand in dismissal.

'Don't worry,' she says. 'It was just scared then, defensive. Wouldn't you react the same way if someone tried to kill you?'

Rima nods slowly as she looks inside. There is no malice in the air today, just a welcoming vibe. But still ...

'Of course,' Nandini continues. 'We didn't know that then. We spent so many sleepless nights thinking the moss would strangle us. We even tried to leave the flat, to find a hotel for a few days, but it wouldn't let all three of us leave. And then, that day when we tried to burn it—'

'What?' Shailesh asks, his voice unnaturally high.

'We were a bit desperate then, and just really tired. This was a few days after Rima ran away—'

'I'm so sorry about that,' Rima softly chimes in.

'No, no. You did nothing wrong. We were all so unsure and apprehensive back then,' Jai Prakash says.

'But still,' Rima continues. 'I should have tried to help.' And then, almost in a whisper, she asks, 'You haven't been kidnapped, have you? The moss isn't holding you hostage?'

Jai Prakash and Nandini look at each other and laugh.

'Of course not,' Jai Prakash says. 'I mean, look at Shallots out there. He is so happy to have some company. Oh, do you know, when we went for our recent vacation, the moss was the one who cared for the cat? It fed him, gave him water, played with him. All by extending its many arms. It even messaged us on its mobile phone (we bought it a Samsung) and sent us pictures and videos of Shallots every day—'

'Wait a second,' Arjun stops Jai Prakash. 'What do you mean by it *sent you pictures and videos*? It can type?'

Nandini smiles. 'You remember how I told you guys that the website selling this moss had great reviews?'

'No. Don't tell me ... that's not possible,' Shailesh says, eyes widening.

Nandini nods. 'I was on the sofa, working, when the moss sent out an arm and typed in the website's URL, and then clicked away till it reached the page with all the reviews. I wrote one, which the moss proofread and posted.'

'It loves being praised,' Jai Prakash adds with an indulgent smile. 'But then, who doesn't?'

Later, when the three guests are at the main door, about to leave, Shailesh brings Jai Prakash to his side and whispers in his ears. 'Are you sure you're okay? You don't want to sell the house or something?'

'Oh no. No. No. I couldn't do that. We love how green the flat is now, how full of life. And the moss helps out a lot, with household chores and—'

'Yes, I saw that. It brought us our lunch out in the balcony today,' Shailesh says, still not quite believing it.

Rima, who has been talking to Arjun and Nandini all this while, takes another look at her surroundings and realises that the moss has somehow *grown* on her.

'Actually,' she says. 'Actually, I really like the vibe of your flat now. It feels like we're inside a forest.' She smiles reassuringly at Nandini.

The very next second, an inquiring arm shoots out from the moss and moves towards a frozen Rima, patting her twice on the head, then merging with the wall once again.

'Aww,' Nandini says. 'It says it likes you too.'

The Forest of Plenty

The Forest of Plenty lies at the heart of the Gaia 232 mothership. People from all over the mothership and the many smaller societyships go there for the 'full nature experience'. Millions of trees are said to reside there, and hundreds and thousands of wild animals. About 100 km² of the total 30,000 km² is unrestricted, and allows families and friends and others to hold picnics or go for a walk or do nothing at all but read under the shade of oaks, willows and maples. An additional 100 km² is set aside inside the Forest of Plenty for agricultural needs. In the remaining 29,800 km², only the forest officials and those with special permission are allowed to enter.

Everything is perfectly laid out.
Everything is perfectly balanced.
On the Gaia 232 and its societyships.

The human population on board the ships is carefully regulated. At all times, the number of humans is strictly between the numbers of 1.5 and 1.7 million. Less than that and a lot of food will get wasted, more than that and there won't be enough food.

A tight balance is maintained. And the Forest of Plenty is at the centre of it all.

When an animal's population crosses the threshold point,

families and friends and others are encouraged to fish and hunt. The kill is later consumed by everyone on board all the ships during the annual 'Boarding Day' anniversary.

Today, in the unrestricted area, a seven-year-old's birthday party is being organised by the Department of Birthdays and Deaths. There are two more birthdays being held on the grounds, but the humans at the centre of those two are older, in their fifties. Their gatherings are more sombre, although there's much laughter there too. The child's party is definitely more colourful and chaotic, with everyone running around everywhere.

The grown-ups, the parents and relatives of the birthday girl, look tired. They are currently using fresh products from the farms, all paid for by the Department of Birthdays and Deaths, and making sandwiches for the fifteen children who seem to have let loose their inner wild animals in the midst of nature.

'I *love* tomatoes,' screams the birthday girl, jumping on the seated adults, escaping with her favourite vegefruit in hand. She bites into it and a stream of juice trickles down her chin. A beast biting into its prey.

'Are you going to let her eat it like that?' a red-haired grown-up, cutting up a cucumber, asks the child's parent.

'Well,' comes the answer, 'there's no way I'm going to run after her.'

'You know,' ventures a barely-an-adult, slicing the sandwiches into two halves. 'I always felt a bit uneasy coming here once I actually knew about this place.'

'What do you mean?' the parent asks. He's finished spreading mayo on the slices of bread.

'Well, you know.' She looks around and notices the line of black-clothed people trailing behind a slow, old man in the distance, walking further into the Forest of Plenty. 'Them. *That.*'

The children wander off. They come close to the edge of the restricted area and spy an old woman in tattered clothes looking lost and confused, walking aimlessly on the other side.

'You're not supposed to be there!' the birthday girl screams.

'Hmm? What? Oh ... yes.' The woman looks around. 'I didn't realise I was this close. I've only been here a few weeks and I'm already lost,' she says, then laughs. She looks at the girl and the fourteen other children around her, and makes a guess. 'Are you here for a birthday party?'

The birthday girl grins. 'I'm seven now.'

'Happy birthday, dear girl,' the old one replies before turning around and heading deeper into the forest.

Most of the children forget about the incident. Indeed, by the end of the day, they are too sleepy to talk about their day at the Forest of Plenty to their parents. But one child remembers and gushes about the weird woman they saw at the party. 'I thought people that old were sent away,' he tells them. 'Away', here, meaning sent out in space, inside a soloship.

The same parents then call the Department of Birthdays and Deaths, and tell them about the incident. Immediately, a team of forest officials start a search for her and, upon finding her, direct her further into the forest.

A month later, she dies, killed by a lioness.

Over time, what's left of her body decays and mixes with the soil, which the forest officials collect and transfer to the farmers, who use the soil to fertilise tomatoes, one of which, a year later, the birthday girl, now eight years old, snatches from her parent's hand and runs around with in the unrestricted area of the Forest of Plenty.

'I *love* tomatoes,' she screams as she bites into it.

She really, truly does love tomatoes.

Whirlwind

A storm's coming. All airships, hot-air balloons and hang-gliders have been grounded for an hour. The sky is a dark grey, bubbling with threat and chaos. The winds are swirling, slow and steady. Ready to strike at any moment. And down below, Haizea is watching it all, her head turned up, a frown of thought clouding her face. She has never seen a storm like this before.

Again, she tries calling her husband.

She gathers the words in her mouth, takes a deep breath and blows out the same sentence she let out five minutes ago. 'Anil, where are you? Are you okay?'

And she gets the same automated reply: *The receiver can't be reached due to the gathering storm.*

Haizea sends messages to his colleagues, even sends a paper airplane to the office receptionist. But all of them get lost in the wind. She is in two minds: should she stay at home and wait for him or go out looking for him? Just then she feels a cool breeze near the back of her head and hears the words, 'Haizea … help … please …'

She tries to hold on to the current, to send a message in return, but it doesn't work.

She must go out. Help her husband.

The wind has picked up. There is dust in the air. Rain might follow as well. But she is safe in her windcheater, which is equipped with instant rope, torch, first aid, energy bars and other items of importance. After she carefully locks the door and puts on her hood, tightening it around the outer edges of her face, Haizea takes out a pair of goggles from an inner pocket and positions them over her eyes. Even then, as she walks further into the storm, she places her right palm in front of her eyes, an instinctive need to protect her eyes, and fights against the fierce winds, getting stronger by the second, as she follows the street into the main road.

Heavy, potent drops of rain begin to fall as she passes the bus stand. There is no one else on the road, not that Haizea can clearly see around her. Shadowy trees and signposts are easy to recognise, but there is a lot of debris as well. Some on the road, most flying in the air in search of a resting ground.

The last time she went looking for her husband in a storm, it wasn't this bad. It was raining heavily, and the comm lines were down again. But a few airships were still operating, and her husband had come home in one of them.

He wasn't too happy she'd gone out in search of him though. He had shouted at her for leaving the house locked, forcing him to wait outside in the lashing rain. 'The neighbours aren't in either! What were you thinking, Haizea? Going off on your own, in the middle of a storm?'

She shakes her head.

This time she wasn't going off on her own. He had *asked* her for help.

Up ahead, Haizea can see the form of another human being. They are walking haphazardly, suggesting an injured left leg. In their hand is a bag of some sort. The winds have started to howl with lost words and screams. So many messages that couldn't be sent. So many people afraid or wounded.

The form is clearer now, and Haizea recognises it to be

that of a colleague of her husband's who travels in the same hot-air bus as him.

'Have you seen Anil?'

But the colleague can't hear her. Even when they are side-by-side, having closed the gap between them upon recognising each other.

Her mouth opens to say something, but the howling wind is all she can hear.

Haizea nods, gives her a thumbs up and moves on.

About ten minutes later the howling wind deposits a few words near her ears: 'Are you looking for Anil?'

Haizea is under a bridge now, waiting in an anti-wind enclosure with the stranded passengers of a deflated aerostat. She has arrived at the eye of the storm, and things are so bad that all everyone can see is the dark brown, gravelly dust in the air. There are no howling winds here, and the visibility is near zero. The shelter under the bridge, designed to combat any kind of natural phenomenon, is the only place Haizea can see things clearly.

She is wondering how long she'll have to wait inside when she feels a cool breeze once again.

'Haizea!'

Just that one word is enough.

She steps out, despite the others telling him to wait, and dives into a dust storm.

'I'm here.' Words appear near her ears, and she suddenly feels pulled towards the right. There, under a huge signboard, a man is struggling desperately.

His eyes are shut, the gravel having gotten into his eyes, but he can sense that someone is helping him.

'Haizea?' he asks.

'Yes,' she responds, lifting the heavy signboard with all her might, allowing him to wriggle out from the gap created. 'How do you know me?'

He is sitting on the ground. His face is cloaked in a layer of dust and grime, but she can still see the look of confusion on his face. 'I'm sorry I don't … If you're not … I mean, wait. Your name is Haizea too?'

'It is.' She helps him stand up. 'And who is your Haizea?'

He laughs, despite the situation. And she feels another sudden pull towards her. 'My girlfriend,' he says. 'Sorry, I think there must have been some cross-connection and … sorry.'

'No problem,' she tells him, looking for an extra pair of goggles in her windcheater. She finds them and swiftly hands them to him.

'Oh, thank you!' he says, and puts them on, opening his eyes for the first time.

At the reveal of his cool grey eyes, she is instantly reminded of the calm, quiet morning she had witnessed ten years ago, when she had gone backpacking in the mountains. The sky was overcast, there was such promise in the air and she had felt a kind of peace she had never experienced before.

He seems to be struck speechless too, staring at her night-black eyes.

'What's your name?' she finally manages to ask.

'Enlil.'

'I studied cloud dynamics too!' he tells her.

They are walking back through the storm, having just bypassed the bridge. He hasn't asked her who she went out to search for, and he hasn't ventured why he was out in the storm. They have found other topics to discuss. Haizea and Enlil, it seems, went to the same college and studied the same subject—five years apart.

'Do you work from home then?' he asks her next.

'I do, yes. Once a month I head to the headquarters to present reports on the clouds in my area. But that's about it.'

'Hmm. And have you always lived here?'

'I have. My husband is from the north though, and he hates this place. Says it's too ... quiet.'

His eyes widen. 'My girlfriend says the same thing! And she is from the north too.'

'Really?' Haizea replies, smiling. She can't stop doing that. She has never felt this happy in someone else's company. 'Sounds like our partners are meant for each other,' she adds, grinning.

He giggles in return.

The storm has dissipated but there are still strong currents in the air, interfering with the comm lines. Haizea couldn't care less though. She is skipping as she walks towards her home. She can still feel his words flowing around her. She has fallen into vortexes before, but never one like this. Head over heels. So in lo—

She stops as he catches sight of her husband in front of her locked house. Drenched, eyes watering due to dust, clothes ruined, one shoe missing, face contorted in anger.

'Oh,' she says. 'You're back.'

A Storm of Stings

'Are you certain there is no other way?'
'Quite certain, my queen.'
'But can't I just—'
'No, your highness. We have to destroy them. They might come after you if word gets out that …'

The queen's advisor is waiting for someone in a secret chamber inside the hive. There is a sense of nervousness in her. She has waited for this moment a long time, planned and made connections, seeded ideas inside others' minds.

She hears the guard before she sees her. The flapping of wings loud in the quiet of the chamber. 'All well, Joy?' she asks as she turns to look at the guard.

'Can't complain,' the guard responds. 'I'm glad I get to stay near home, yet fly around outside. It's an easy job, to be honest.'

'Hmm. Good. Good.'

'So … why did you call me here?'

'Ah, yes,' the queen's advisor says. 'Well, the thing is … I have a job for you.'

It's pitch dark outside, most of the hive's residents are asleep, when the queen quietly creeps out of the back entrance with the advisor guiding her.

A Storm of Stings

'The guard is elsewhere?'

'Yes,' her advisor says. 'I sent her on a stupid errand—said you wished to smell some pollen, and since the worker bees are strict about their rules, we couldn't really ask them.'

'And she bought it?'

'Needed some convincing, but I told her how all queens spend their entire lives cooped up inside, flying out just once, to mate.'

The queen buzzed with laughter. 'That's a good answer. And it's true too. I do get bored inside.'

They are right at the gate. The queen is a bit anxious. 'I'm still not sure.'

'There is no other way,' comes the answer.

The queen flies carefully, making sure not to draw attention. She is guilty too, for what she's decided to do is the most selfish thing a mother could do. But this was about her *survival*. If the hive got to know her eggs were rotten, they would immediately kill her by balling. If her advisor hadn't noticed that something was wrong with the eggs, and soon after come up with a plan to fix it, she doesn't know what she would have done.

Luckily, her pheromones are still intact.

So, she moves further and further away from the nest until she hears the buzz of unknown wings. They sound strong, and the queen is relieved. No chance now that the eggs will be weak. But as she nears the source of the sound, she feels more alarm than calm. All around her, quite suddenly, are hornets upon hornets.

'Are you on your way to ... to the hive?' she asks.

'We are,' they say in unison.

'Oh.' Should she back out? She feels very uneasy. And shouldn't the hornets already been at the nest by now, ready to attack? 'Aren't you ... aren't you late?'

'Late for what?' they ask.

The queen is confused. 'Didn't my advisor tell you? That when I'm ... away, you had to attack and ... and kill the eggs?'

'You mean *your* eggs? You're the mother.'

'That's right,' she answers, wings dropping a bit. 'I am. Unfortunately, the eggs aren't ... right, and if the others find out about it—'

'How do you know that?' a hornet right in front of her asks. 'How do you know the eggs aren't right?'

'Well, my advisor said that they were growing wrong and—'

'You believed her?' another hornet asks.

'I don't understand,' the queen says. 'Why would my advisor lie?'

'Power,' the hornets collectively reply. 'The only thing that drives this world.'

She is quite aware now that this whole outing was a miscalculation on her part, that she should have never trusted her advisor. And that soon all her healthy, perfectly normal eggs were going to be destroyed because of her foolishness.

They start closing in on her. The queen knows she should try to fight or run, but she hovers, frozen in spot. 'But why are *you* doing this? What could you possibly gain from all this?'

The hornets reply as they prepare themselves for an attack. 'Why are *we* doing this? Because there's nothing else we love than some royal jelly, and some pure, uncontrollable chaos.'

Loy, the queen's advisor, wasn't the only one to survive the day the newly hatched queen stepped out of her cell in the royal birth chamber. The moment they heard her piping, a few of them cut open their cells and escaped the hive. Most, though, piped back. And the queen found her rivals and stung them to death. Knowing she wasn't as strong, Loy quietly left her cell and let instincts guide her to an empty chamber. She stole bread when the workers were busy, and rid herself of the queenly pheromones brought on by a diet of royal jelly.

She waited until a few days had passed before joining the workers. And when the time came for an advisor to be chosen, she put her name forward and won every round of interview. She knew every single detail of a queen's duties and responsibilities. How could she not?

The moment she became the queen's advisor, Loy began to plan. Carefully, over the next two months, she built trust and deceit, and convinced the queen to go forward with her plan. And now. Now. Now she was finally ready to become what she was born to be.

'Sisters of the hive,' she screams in the main hall, catching everyone's attention. 'I come bearing some terrible news. Last night, our queen left her quarters and went out in the night. She hasn't come back yet, and I … I fear the worst.'

A buzz of energy goes through the hive.

'Is she dead?'

'What will happen to us?'

'We'll need to select a new queen!'

'It will take days for a new queen to emerge.'

'What will we do till then?'

The voices die out as everyone starts to sense threat nearby. There is a loud buzz of wings, growing louder and louder. Muted panic begins to rise up in the hive, and Loy quickly hides away in a secret chamber she had prepared for this very purpose.

And then the hornets come into view.

They crash inside, maiming and killing ruthlessly on their way to the royal birth chamber. They eat the eggs, steal most of the royal jelly surrounding the cells and leave. Not once do they say anything, or explain why they attacked the hive.

Loy, who has heard everything from her hiding place, feels excited as she thinks of the next step in her plan—how she will volunteer to go out on a mating flight and become their official queen. Before that, she must do something else. She steps out with a concerned face as she assesses the damage: the broken cells, the injured and dead workers, and the loss of royal jelly. She tries to control her pheromones, to not let her glee escape. She is successful too, until another alarm goes up in the hive.

'A single hornet is approaching!'

Loy is confused. That was not the deal. What were they up to? She thinks of going back into hiding when suddenly cries of anguish fill the air. As more and more workers head to the entrance, the sound only grows stronger. Loy heads out too, forcing her way through the crowd, and is shocked beyond words to see the decapitated head of the former queen on the wooden platform at the entrance.

'We must attack them!'

'But so many of us will die!'

'Why did the queen go out at all?'

'If only she had stayed put.'

'Now the eggs are gone too.'

'Oh, what will we do?'

'We can't just take decisions like this. We need *someone*, we need a queen!'

Loy is gearing up to offer her services, when one of the workers chimes up: 'What about the queen's advisor? She knows everything, and she is the closest thing we have to a leader.'

'All in favour of Loy as the new queen, say "Aye!",' shouts out a voice.

'AYE!'

'All not in favour, say "nay". And tell us why we should not choose her as the queen.'

Nothing happens for a few seconds, and then comes the weary voice of Joy, the guard who had been sent away. 'Nay,' her voice rings out true. 'For she murdered our queen!'

Whispers and pipings fill the air inside the hive.

'How dare you?' Loy asks. 'Who are you to accuse me of such a heinous crime? That too when we just saw a hornet deliver our beloved former queen's head?'

Joy stumbles through the air, her wings battered, her pheromones dripping with anger. 'Oh yes, the hornets,' she says. 'They told me everything! How you conspired with them, how you convinced the queen to go out and mate again after you told her that her eggs were rotten. The hornets told me everything!'

'This is absurd!' Loy says.

'And as to who I am?' Joy continues. 'I am a hardworking, dedicated member of this hive you sent out to her death because you needed the coast clear for the queen to leave the nest, to her death.'

'None of that makes sense!'

'Doesn't it?' Joy questions. She is face-to-face with Loy now. 'Tell me, do the others know that you are the queen's sister? That you escaped and hid, waited till you could join the workers? That you manoeuvred your way into the queen's inner circle?'

The energy inside the hive suddenly changes at these words. They each try to remember if Loy had ever been their cellmate at the general birth chamber, but no one can remember.

'That's true! Loy just appeared in our lives out of nowhere! But I just assumed ...'

'I thought someone else must know her, even though I didn't.'

'There are so many of us that I never questioned her background.'

Loy tries to come up with an excuse even as she feels a rise in temperature inside the hive. Were the workers slowly closing in on her? She can't tell.

'So what if I was the queen's sister? I loved her, she was my own blood,' Loy tries to reason with everyone. 'Is it wrong to want to survive? To try to live?'

'No,' Joy says, echoing the energy of the workers who have now surrounded Loy. 'No. But it is a crime to kill a queen who is in her prime.'

The sun rises and the birds call out. Animals wake up and dream of all the food they will have today. And two beekeepers, suited up and hands covered in gloves, move towards the row of wooden apiary in the garden. They stop at each tree-station and check the build-up of honey. They check ten hives without any issues, but stop at the eleventh one, and stare.

On the platform are two dead bees. One of them looks to be the queen, even though only her head is on the platform. The other looks like a worker bee, but seems to have been killed by balling.

'What the hell happened last night?' one dumbstruck beekeeper asks the other, who throws his hands in the air, speechless.

Solastalgic

For the longest time, all I wanted to do was run away from home. I couldn't stand all the grey around me—the skies that hadn't poured in months, the people who had lost joy in life and the buildings that were built with beige bricks.

Once, when I was eleven, I did escape: to the city. I don't remember where all I went and what all I saw, I only have dreamlike memories of the lights, the bright advertorial holograms, the plastic smiles of people no matter where I walked and the tall, canopy-like skyscrapers that stood unyielding and unimpressed.

I spent a few hours there until I started to feel alone and scared, and I went back—into the stern arms of my parents—with the determination that the moment I was able to, I would move to a better place. But now that I'm here, on a planet called Farearth, I'm filled with an immense longing for, and an immeasurable guilt about, having left Earth to fend for itself.

My partner doesn't think that way. He says it was necessary for us to leave, for all of us to leave. 'We thought we were gods,' he told me one evening, when I remarked that I didn't like the shade of sunlight on Farearth, that there was an artificial tone to it. 'We behaved like we owned Earth, when in fact we were like the plaque that slowly builds up and eats away at the enamel. By the time we realised we were the root problem, it was too late. Extraction was the only way out.'

We were sent out in batches of ten thousand over a period of a hundred years. A planet within the boundaries of Milky Way had already been selected, scoped and prepared as the new home for humanity and whatever else they may bring with them. For ten years, it was known simply as Planet B, until someone online began calling it Far Earth, and that somehow resulted in the Head of the Rehoming Department leading a vote to rename the planet Farearth.

There was no hue and cry over the collective decision to leave Earth. No riots or violence of any kind.

For some, there was only a great sadness, a cruel acceptance of the fact. The flash floods, followed by extended periods of drought, the sea that had claimed nearly a tenth of the coastlines and the severely hot and freezing cold conditions had meant that, if we stayed on, we would kill ourselves and the entire planet. It didn't help that our numbers had drastically declined—for the aforementioned reasons, as well as the fact that more and more of us were being born infertile.

Still, a lot of us were excited too. I was one of them. I couldn't wait to reach our new home and start afresh. I had never really felt rooted in any place, so I didn't think I'd have any problems adjusting to Farearth. After all, it was a bigger and greener planet.

What could go wrong?

'I don't understand what their deal is.'

'Who? What deal?' I ask, not looking away from the screen. The first batch of the day is about to arrive, and I am checking the list of new residents.

'These ... Solastalgic people,' Darun continues. He is

my assistant; he should be keeping an eye on the numbers too, but is looking at some social media app on his phone instead.

I turn to glance at him. 'What about them?'

His gaze turns ceilingwards in thought. 'Well, the name itself is so ...'

'Sophisticated?' I offer.

'... bland,' he finishes. 'It doesn't really *say* what they want, what they stand for. Do you know?'

'Me?'

'You're the one with a government official for a partner.'

'Oh. Well, we don't really talk about these things ... Although, as far as I know, the word "solastalgia" refers to the feeling a person gets when they see the environmental damage in the place they grew up. They feel sad, distraught—'

Darun snorts. 'I know what the word means. I just think something like, I don't know, Earth Warriors could have been better. Straight and direct.'

'Earth Warriors?'

Darun continues, ignoring me. 'I actually liked their initial posts, where they talked about the collective guilt we all felt leaving our home behind, and how we need to be more careful about Farearth and how we treat it. But now, it just feels like they are saying the same thing over and over again. When will they really *do* something?'

I don't answer, for I'm done checking the list, and it's time to go out and receive the new residents. They'll land in about ten minutes.

'Let's go,' I tell Darun and head out.

Later, as I let my slideshoes walk me home, my eyes fall on the bushes and grass lining the roads. They are all native to this planet, and are all harmless. And, I guess, charming in their own way. But to my eyes, they look like those plastic plants some people used to decorate their homes with back on Earth.

Although we were allowed to bring plants and pets with us to Farearth, I didn't bring any. I could never bond with an animal, and I had never managed to keep a potted plant alive in my little Earthian apartment. But there are others who did, and more and more I'll see a dog or a cat or sometimes even a fox out on a walk. Largely though, we've left all our flora and fauna behind. We couldn't bring a blue whale with us, could we? And anyway, we have the genomes of every possible life that lived on Earth, even those that had gone extinct by the time we left.

We have manufactured quite a few of them, and created zones and quarters for the wild ones. Those that had shown comfort in a human settlement on Earth have been allowed the same access here.

One more thing: we have dinosaurs too.

I was quite surprised when I heard my partner speak about it at home while feeding our daughter, who was a year old then. It was the early days of our life on this planet, we had arrived only a month ago.

'A dinosaur?' I had repeated, dumbstruck.

'*Dinosaurs*, actually,' he had corrected, grinning.

'But ... why?'

He had sighed, wiped his hands with a towel on the table in front of him and faced me with a solemn expression.

'It took us a long time to understand why we had lost our way on Earth, why we thought we could do anything and not face any consequences,' he had said.

'Capitalism?'

'Sure,' he said. 'Money and greed took over our lives. And yes, in order to make gains in the present, everything about the future was forgotten. But what truly ruined us was fear, or our lack of it.'

My partner paused as he cleaned our daughter's face, and placed her in my arms. 'Yes,' he said, taking her bowl to the sink. 'Yes, we feared the wild and abstract things like failure, but there was not one true object that filled us up with cold, dark terror. There was an absence of a primal fear that would keep us all in check.'

Filled with dawning horror, I put our daughter in the hovering, indoor pram and stood to face him. 'Then dinosaurs—'

'They'll be restricted to their own quarters, of course. Farearth is large enough for us to assign a portion of it to them. But just the knowledge of them being on the same world as us, living and breathing close by, an open threat ready to devour us ... that is enough to make us stay within limits.'

'The government couldn't think of anything better?' I had asked, the absurdity of the whole idea hitting me, annoying me. 'Dinosaurs, really?'

'A lot of research has gone into this,' he answered, softly dragging the pram to our daughter's room. 'You'll see; the dinos will work.'

The first batch was reserved for the builders and the engineers, the farmers and the scientists. They came and laid the foundation for the capital, Meerko, where we now live and work. Two more towns were added over the next ten years, and a few villages too for those who wanted a quieter life. Just over a million humans had survived over the years, and there was no need for any more construction. The houses and apartments were ready and waiting.

As was I.

I arrived with the second batch of residents. Being single and unattached, I was allotted a partner, and we were given a child to raise and care for. Her parents had perished in a flash flood. There were many family units like ours, manufactured by the government to help us adjust to life on Farearth together as a unit of three or four as well as a larger collective of a million.

Very early on, I had started to feel that unity. On a set day every decade, we were woken up from our cryosleep—it took us five decades to reach here—to undergo health check-ups. My co-passengers and I looked on with immense horror and sadness as we read about how progressively bad things had got over each ten-year gap.

Entire countries had been destroyed, some species had been erased and the world had come to a standstill.

There were many like me on Farearth who were filled with an unimaginable guilt, who often cried themselves to sleep, distraught at what they had lost. No matter how big, beautiful and joyous this new planet seemed to be, it only made us reflect on all that we had lost.

The government didn't like such discussions, of course, so we met in secret. We talked about our childhoods and everything we could remember from the good old days. We wrote everything down, fearing that we—and others—might forget. Soon, we started to share our thoughts on social media, on flyers posted on walls, and we selected a name for our little group. We picked it because our brains were searching for solace, and we were steeped in nostalgia. We liked the meaning of the word too.

'Are you sure this is the right thing to do?' Aegyl asks. The meeting hasn't started yet. The two of are in one corner of the room.

'We cannot step down now,' I say. 'We have already spent a lot of time and energy into this. This is something we have to do, or at least try.'

'Yes, but,' she replies. 'What about Farbek and Viordoe?'

I don't know. I say that out loud as well. 'It's unexpected, but ... but,' I take a deep breath, 'we *have* to move ahead.'

Aegyl nods, though she is not completely convinced, and moves to the front of the room to announce my presence and introduce me to the newcomers. Every month, we've been adding two or more people to the Solastalgic. Every new batch that lands brings us more guilty minds.

'Welcome, everyone,' I say. 'To those who have joined us for the first time today, and those that have been with us for a longer time, I welcome you all.'

There is some polite applause.

'As you know, we've used this forum to talk about our hopes and dreams, our guilt and nostalgia—every thought we have about Earth. But for some time, a few of us have been feeling inadequate, that all we were doing was talking. There was a need in us to actually *do* something. Although we were all ferried to this world on promises and urgency, we never quite acclimatised to leaving our home. We never quite understood the weight of our actions, and how we never really helped Mother Earth through her toughest time.'

'What are you trying to say?' someone from the audience asks. A sceptic, or someone particularly cautious.

'I can't reveal the exact plans now, but soon you'll hear of a most outrageous incident, and you'll know that was us!'

'Are Farbek and Viordoe also involved? Is this why they are missing?' another voice asks. I can identify this one—it's Liuo, Farbek's friend from college.

'Yes, they are,' I answer.

'And *where* are they?' Liuo continues.

Words get caught up in my throat and I cough. 'We aren't sure, but I think they might be lying low for the time being.'

'So the government caught them?' someone else asks. His arms are folded, his forehead has developed a frown.

'No, I don't thin—'

'I eavesdropped on two government officials in a café yesterday, and they said they had fed two traitors to the dinosaurs,' Ilop says, standing up. Her eyes are wide in terror. 'I thought it was a joke, I didn't make the connection then, but ... Oh, what a horrible way to die! Nothing could be worse.'

A cacophony of outburst erupts and drowns out Aegyl's two-word dismissal: 'That's absurd.'

I try to calm them, with shushes and a couple of 'Please listen to me' and 'Please sit down' to those who have stood up in agitation. But when nothing works, I break out a swift, sharp whistle and catch their attention.

My voice is low and commanding as I tell them: 'The government has allotted us everything in this new life—a partner, a child, a house, a job. We cannot let them choose the life we want for us. We cannot let them stop us, when all we want is to help our dying Earth.'

After I read a bedtime story to our daughter, I tell my partner I'm going to meet some friends and will return quite late. His glasses and face focused on the book in front of him, he only emits a small 'hmm', and then reminds me to take the second set of keys. 'I don't think I'll be awake when you return.'

It all happens quite easily. I get my little group into the landing office using my employee card and type in my clearance code to gain entrance into the parking area. There are twelve ships waiting for us, to take us back home.

'Wow,' Ilop says, as she looks around. She volunteered for this mission after my speech, said she wanted to overcome her fears. 'These ships are *so beautiful*.'

Aegyl agrees, and I tell her to switch on the spotlights.

The moment she does that, the doors open once again and in marches my partner with a group of twenty security guards behind him.

I am frozen in place, my mouth is wide open and I try to think of something to say. *Anything.*

'You!'

'Me,' he confirms.

'What are you ...?'

'What made you think taking a ship back to Earth would solve things?' he replies instead, walking towards me. 'You would have died most assuredly. All fifteen of you. It's not the same place that you left. There are still years to go before the planet begins to heal, which it can only do *without us*. And why do you think *you* can save it? Maybe, a long time ago, when we first realised how we were harming our planet, with our oil leaks and gas emissions, and fire and smoke, and needless slaughter of animals. Maybe *then*, we could have learnt from our mistakes and turned back. But we didn't. And now there is nothing left for us to do. We have to let nature run its course.'

He is right in front of me now, his face is cold and clear. 'Do you understand?'

I look around me, at the people who have followed me to their doom. 'Did you know that I was …?'

He smiles. 'A little bit of rebellion is always encouraged.'

'And … and Farbek and Viordoe? Did you catch them too?'

'You'll see,' he answers, aggravatingly, and motions the security guards to arrest us.

All of us are pushed into a buscopter and are lifted out of Meerko. We are huddled together on a single, long seat, while security agents and government officials stare at us from a similar seat opposite. One of them catches Ilop's eye and she gasps: 'You're the guy I saw at the café! You were the one who said that they feed traitors to—'

'But you didn't listen, did you?' the man in question replies, dramatically sighing.

'He's just joking,' I whisper to Ilop. There is no way they would do such a thing. I think.

'Oh yeah?' she whispers back. 'Then why are we moving further and further away from Meerko into wilder regions?'

I turn my head and look out the window. She was

right. We seemed to drawing closer to dense forests and vast grasslands. And then, suddenly, I see *them*. Massive animals, ambling about in the space allotted to them. Alive and well after centuries of being dead.

Aegyl, on my other side, begins to sob quietly.

'Doesn't our marriage mean anything to you?' I bite through my words, unable to look at him clearly through my tear-addled eyes.

He doesn't say anything, although there is an amused expression on his face. 'Let me know when it's over,' he tells a person in a brown hazmat suit. And then he leaves.

Some of us are crying, bawling, screaming, dragging our feet on the ground as we are led towards a domed building. I have no feelings left inside me, I am limp and still in shock when they open the gates and let us inside.

There is still ground beneath us—mud and dirt—but the surroundings are more like that of a lab, with technicians and scientists milling about in their coats and hazmat suits. All of us are handed our own suit and given safety goggles as well.

It's the most confused I've ever been in my life.

'Where are we going?' I ask the security guard clutching my arm, guiding me through the building, but the woman says nothing. The others, behind me, are asking similar questions to receive similar answers.

We move deeper into the building, away from the lab. There is an awful smell in the air when we reach a darkened, cemented hallway. The stench only grows stronger as we move further along the way.

'Here it is,' the guard says, releasing me at the solitary door in the hall.

I open the door, curiosity taking over, and look around: all around the room there are massive tanks, and people are coming in through a door on the right with wheelbarrows filled to the brim. They are walking in and shovelling the contents into the tanks, and heading back again. The smell is horrible, and all of us clamp our noses and mouths in disgust. We have a fair idea of what the wheelbarrows are full of.

'You'll get used to it,' one of the guards offers just as two hazmat-covered figures enter the room, turn to look at us and wave before getting on with their work.

'Is that ...?' I ask.

'Farbek and Viordo,' Ilop replies in a monotone.

A person who looks to be in charge of the whole exercise heads towards us and hands each one of us a small shovel from a locker next to the door.

'Extra wheelbarrows are outside. There will be a guide who'll help you gather the deposits. Don't worry, we don't keep any carnivores here. You'll be fine, and you'll be allowed to go home only when we think you've done an adequate job. It could be days or months. Hopefully not years,' he says, guffawing.

'And why do we ... have to do this?' Aegyl asks.

'Well, how else will you get electricity in the towns? This is the best bio fuel there is. The people out there think solar power is driving the economy, but it's actually this—pure, unadulterated, top quality dino shit and its wonderful, wonderful methane that's bringing electricity to your homes.'

'So this is what happens to anyone who—'

'Does illegal stuff? Exactly!' the man jovially exclaims. 'Some are our employees, of course, so that there's always a permanent team shovelling shit. But most are people like you! Now, news of this facility will surely get out sooner or later. But till then, it'll be our little secret!' He mimes zipping his mouth with the tips of his thumb and index finger, and then beckons us towards the door that leads to the outside. 'Let's go!' he says excitedly. 'Come on, there's a lot of work to do!'

A few days into this exercise, when our nasal cavities give up telling us where we are and what we are doing, and when all we dream about is being crushed under the weight of a dinosaur's paw, Ilop collapses at the end of a particularly gruelling day and says, 'I was wrong. *This* is much, much worse.'

The Golden Bird

The Delhi Zoo is no labyrinth. It is, instead, five neat concentric circles, each holding like-minded animals—airborne, waterborne and landborne (divided further into carnivores, herbivores and omnivores). But the beast that rests and prowls at the centre, in her domed cage, could very well be considered a mythical monster. Nur has golden, iridescent scales from her head to her tail, massive legs that end in sharp talons, a wingspan so vast it could shelter two elephants on either side, and a belly so full of fire and heat and loathing that no man or woman could stand in front of her and hope to survive. Nur is, after all, a dragon.

Though she clearly lives and breathes, and those of her kind have been spotted in mountainous regions for thousands of years, there is still an element of otherworldliness to her existence. Books and films that feature her ilk are termed fantasy. It seems fantastical to people that something as intimidating and awe-inspiring as Nur could be flying over their heads.

Though people from all over the world come to see her, the 'Golden Bird of India', the moment they leave the zoo and head to their houses or hotel rooms, the entire experience dissolves into a dream for them. They are dazed for a few days afterwards; their own lives don't feel real.

Standing in the queue outside the dragon's enclosure, Riya feels restless and nervous. She closes her fists and opens them, and places her weight on one foot and then the other. Every day since she moved to Delhi, Riya has been wondering if she should visit the zoo. Almost everyone in her class has seen Nur. It's almost like a rite of passage to them, another step in the path towards adulthood, another barrier broken now that they are eighteen.

But still, Riya feels young and small, afraid to meet a dragon for the first time in her life. She closes her eyes in an effort to calm her nerves, and catches snatches of conversations all around her.

'Isn't it amazing how some traders just happened upon her in Uzbekistan? She was still an egg then, you know, when she was found and presented to Babur?'

'And then that savage—'

'Mughal emperor.'

'He wasn't one *then*. He was a barbarian who invaded India—'

'Stop it. How many times have I told you to—'

'I actually saw a video the other day which explained how Babur brought Islam to the country and forced everyone to convert.'

'Really? He forced *everyone* to convert? Are you sure about that? Are you sure there even *was* an India then? That the entire subcontinent wasn't made up of small kingdoms?'

Riya moves on. Conversations like these infuriate her.

'Didn't the British try to ship Nur to England after the Revolt of 1857?' someone else was saying.

'They did? I don't know. Did anyone survive the attempt?'

'Some did, yes. She sent them a warning—a vision—and told them she was going to burn them all. Many heeded her message and escaped, but those that stayed … well, you can guess what might have happened.'

Riya focuses on another conversation, where three people were talking about the dragon's diet. The consensus seemed to be on a monthly consumption of three goats, one buffalo and five chickens. She is surprisingly soothed by how those behind her in the line are relaxed yet excited to see Nur. Sure, they aren't in her position, right at the front of the queue, near the door, next to which the tour guide is looking at his phone. He is leaning against a tall table that has piles of guidebooks and sunglasses on them.

She looks at the light above the door, the bright red that stopped them all in their tracks, and notices the guide tucking his mobile back into his pocket.

'A few minutes more,' he softly says, noticing her restlessness.

'Is it ... is she ... they say she can be very scary?' Riya asks. 'Is that true?'

The man, middle-aged and balding, smiles. 'Yes, she most definitely is. But she is not like the lions and crocodiles outside, who'll harm you only to defend themselves. Nur is different; her mind is like yours or mine. She is capable of jealousy, anger and terrible spite.'

'Spite?'

He lowers his voice. 'Wouldn't you be unhappy if you were locked up for hundreds of years, especially when you had the ability to fly?'

'So,' Riya begins, closely looking at him, 'you think she should be free?'

'I will never say such a thing in public. I don't want to end up in jail.' He laughs, before turning serious again and asking her, 'You'll be careful, won't you? Nur is known to ... make connections with sympathetic people. No matter what visions she sends you, don't get carried away, okay?'

Riya nods.

'There's a section on her telepathic powers in the guidebook,' he says, handing her one from the table next to him. 'Do read it,' he adds, as he picks up nine more guidebooks.

As he moves past her to hand out guidebooks to the rest of the visitors and warn them just as he had warned her, Riya brings the book to her nose and breathes in, hoping for a hint of smokiness or some kind of distinctive dragon scent, even though she has no idea what the beasts smell like. All she can tell is that the pages are newly printed.

She opens the book right at the start, to the table of contents, and finds a chapter simply titled 'Visions'. She flips through the pages and finds her destination, and sees paragraph upon paragraph about how some ancient civilisations corresponded with the dragons. Detrimentally in the case of some Aztecs, who misinterpreted a warning vision against the possibility of widespread death and took it upon themselves to commit mass suicide. How the flying beasts rarely ever came out to meet humans after that one incident and used their camouflaging abilities to stay hidden from the eyes of men and women alike. And how Nur herself was a last-ditch effort on their part to see if a fruitful association could be made with the bipeds.

This is largely conjecture, of course, says a note at the end of the chapter, *reliably inferred from oral histories, written tablets and buried bodies, and hindered by the fact that the only dragon we know by name refuses to offer any insight.*

There is a smile on Riya's face as she finishes reading the lines, as she moves to the other sections. At one particular page she stops. The lettering here is all in gold—unlike the other pages where the words are in dull grey or black. 'The Golden Bird' declares the title, and the text goes on to explain in great detail how the golden epithet was first given to Nur, but was later transferred to the lands beyond the Indus, to Pakistan, India and Bangladesh. *Of course,* says one short paragraph, *it helped that the region was extremely rich at that time, and traders from all over the world were eager to do business with the many kingdoms that populated the three countries.*

Riya is about to read more, but the light above her beeps green, and the guide jogs up from the end of the queue to open the door with his card, and say one last time: 'Please be careful around Nur. If she likes you, she'll send you a message, which can be anything. Don't be fooled by it, don't fall prey to her charms. Remember,' he adds, as they step into a dark tunnel one by one, and he hands them each a pair of sunglasses, 'she's been on Earth far longer than any of you, and is a lot smarter than she looks.'

There used to be a nineteenth-century painting by the English artist Charles Harris, which showed how Nur was captured by the British in 1811. It was titled 'The Taming of the Flying Worm' and depicted the East India Company forces using ropes and nets to overpower the dragon.

The painting existed for exactly forty-six years before someone had the bright idea to mark the occasion of defeating the rebellion of 1857 with a photo of Nur right next to her painting. It was supposed to signify the death of Mughal rule and the complete control of India by the British crown.

On that fateful day, the dragon—her wings and legs bound—graciously allowed the photographer to click the envisioned picture in her well-lit dungeon before casually turning her head to the side and burning the painting to a crisp.

That photograph is the only evidence that the painting ever existed.

The tunnel they are in is dimly lit, forcing them all into silence. There's not even whispers among the lot of them now. Up ahead, at the end of the tunnel, in tune with the saying, there is a bright light beckoning them. The floor beneath their feet is a rough, textured tile imitating dry mud, while the walls are a pale yellow, with flecks of gold here and there.

It is a short walk, the path ahead is maybe half a kilometre long. When they emerge from it, an even deeper quietude descends on the group. They are in an enclosed, red-carpeted ring around the dragon's dome from which daylight is streaming in. The area is completely empty, barring the information touchscreens that are placed near the curved, off-white walls. In front of them, beyond the glasses that separate the beast from the humans, there is no movement save for the leaves that sway in the gentle breeze. There are plenty of those to go around—trees and plants and bushes—in the massive football stadium-sized home built for Nur.

No one comes and goes from the dome, apart from the birds who come in through the metallic net above. Mostly pigeons, either dumb or suicidal, hopping around on the rocky surface of the enclosure. There are only three of them now.

As Riya slowly walks in a circle, she chances upon them in a sparser section of the dome. A part of her wants to shoo them away, but another part doesn't want to disturb the natural way of life. Still, her eyes are drawn to them, and she moves closer to the glass to look at them clearly.

For a long time nothing happens. Nur is nowhere to be found, and the visitors start to talk among themselves, bored and disappointed. There is no guarantee, they'd been told at the ticket counter, that they would get to see the dragon during their allotted time of one hour.

'I think she enjoys watching us when we can't watch her in return,' the woman at the counter had told Riya.

It does seem that way to Riya now. She suddenly feels a pair of eyes on her, on everyone around her, gathered to look at the pigeons inside. She carefully moves her head around to see if she can spot something. A glint of gold catches her eye to the left, and she steps back in alarm. Behind her, the rest of the group gasp and swear, catching the same scene.

The very next second, a river of steam flows towards

the pigeons from the left and disturbs their rest. On reflex, the birds spread their wings and take flight, moving in the direction of the netting. They are nearly there too when a burst of flame comes out of nowhere and burns them in an instant.

Riya and the others, captivated and scared, rush back to the wall, unable to move any further.

'Oh my god,' someone exclaims.

'Is that …?'

'Yes, yes, it has to be.'

There is a shimmering in the air as two pigeons disappear one after another. And the third falls to the ground, where it had been alive only a few seconds ago. There is no sound, no warning of any kind as Nur slowly reveals herself, flying leisurely to the ground. Her wings glide with such ease that it seems like she is sliding on ice rather than swooping through air. Her claws, unclenched, are twitching with mischief, and her eyes—black, with a ring of gold around them—are aimed right at her visitors who have all quickly put on their sunglasses in the brilliance of her presence.

After she lands with a quiet elegance, she gently nudges the dead bird towards the glass and points her head, once towards the pigeon and then towards them.

'Is she threatening us or is she offering us food?' someone nervously asks, as the beasts bares her pointy teeth at them in the manner of a grin.

But she only waits a minute or two before tilting her head to the side, as if saying, 'Oh, well,' and eating the third pigeon. As she slowly chews the roasted bird, which she could easily swallow in one go, Nur looks at each of her visitors, her gaze resting more intensely on a few individuals. As a group, they all hold their breath, clinging to the wall, unable to move for fear of Nur breaking the glass and lunging at them, even though they all know it was bullet-proof and unbreakable.

In a moment, Nur comes upon Riya. She bypasses the dark shades and looks directly into her eyes, and Riya feels cold all over. From her toes to her ears. She can't feel the ground beneath her feet anymore, nor the wall at the back.

And then the feeling is gone. Nur has moved on to the person standing next to Riya.

Thousands have fallen prey to Nur's visions over the years. Most have taken it in their stride and have not dwelt on her messages, but others haven't been able to stop themselves from acting according to what they believed were Nur's wishes.

They have tried to destroy the metallic netting, disable the security system of the entire zoo and even tried to kill the guards and guides—all in an attempt to free the dragon.

Every one of the miscreants has been caught and jailed, and it is because of them that the government has been forced to pass a bill to make discussions about freeing Nur a punishable offence.

In the run-up to the hundredth Independence Day celebrations, rumours abound about Nur being present at the Red Fort, the erstwhile Mughal residence, for the prime minister's address. Many say she'll be used to light a massive lamp that will be kept burning for an entire year.

The government denies it all, but then the day comes, and Nur is standing on a tricolour platform, next to the dignitaries' glass-enclosed stage. There is a collar around her neck, which is attached to the chains on her claws. Her wings, Riya is surprised to note, are untamed and free.

There is a second when the camera pans to show the dragon's handlers, and Riya thinks she sees the tour guide from the zoo among them. But the screen shifts focus to the guests gathered at the function—the businessmen, athletes and actors who are sitting on the side in open air—before zooming in on the face of the sunglasses-clad prime minister, a narcissistic woman whose road to power was driven by nothing but hypernationalism and anti-Muslim rhetoric.

Riya scrunches up her nose as she looks at her, wishing she would stop talking, but the woman is a better actor than most in Bollywood. She knows how to chew every word that comes out of her mouth, trying to elicit emotions out of her audience, the large crowd that has gathered outside the gates of the Mughal monument.

'Brothers and sisters,' she is saying, 'it's time for our dear Nur to light the lamp, the "chirag" of this great nation. This flame will be kept burning till the next Independence Day as a mark of our eternal gratitude to god.'

Riya sits up straighter in her sofa chair, clutching the armrest in her hands. She can't quite explain it, but she has the feeling that something is about to happen. She watches as Nur walks up to the lamp, and nothing happens. The dragon opens her mouth, breathes fire and lights the lamp, and nothing happens. She walks back to her platform, extremely slow, and still *nothing happens*.

The camera is focused on her face. Her golden scales shining extra bright on a warm, sunny day. Everyone watching the scene on their laptops, phones and televisions is able to notice the glimmer in her eye, the subtle tilt of her head towards the glass-enclosed stage. Suddenly, she turns her head to the side and looks at the prime minister, blowing steam from her nostrils.

Next, as Riya gasps at each successive action, Nur picks up the chain and breaks it with a fierce tug, then uses her front left claw to pull away her collar and lift off from the platform. It all happens so quickly that no one reacts for a few seconds. Soon, the area erupts in screams and cries, amid which bodyguards rush to protect government officials and seated guests. There is a look of such complete disbelief on the PM's face as she is moved to a more secure location that Riya can't help but laugh.

There are a few seconds when there is no feed, when

the camera falls to the ground. But the operators quickly switch to the perspective of a drone flying above the Red Fort, and are therefore able to capture the following scenes.

A mix of policemen, army officers and security guards try to control the situation by firing rounds at Nur, but her scales keep her safe. She doesn't even pay them any attention, instead hovering and watching the chaotic repercussions of her actions. There is a grin on her face, not unlike the one Riya saw at the zoo. Experimentally, she lets out a short stream of flame, which makes the people down below even more desperate. Even the crowds outside are in a panic and close to a stampede.

Nur sees them all as she swoops down, only a few feet above the people, her wings spread wide. In another second, she flies high up again, and her camouflage kicks in. She disappears mid-air.

There have been rare sightings of dragons in all mountainous or hilly regions of India—the Western Ghats, the Nilgiris, the Aravallis—but the beasts are said to enjoy living in the Himalayas the most. They love the cold, how sparse the human populations are, but from whom they can source chickens, goats and cows once in a while.

The villagers and townspeople, although inconvenienced by the stealthy attacks, respect the dragons for their might and discipline. They could easily feast on the people, but they don't. They keep to themselves and practice restraint.

In the months following Nur's escape, the papers are full of articles about how it was all 'planned' beforehand, and that the prime minister had wished to mark the occasion by freeing the dragon. There is not a word about how her government was the one to criminalise discussions about freeing Nur. And only a small section is devoted to Nur herself or where she might be.

A year later, there is hardly any mention of dragons

in the media. New issues crop up; the government finds new ways and reasons to imprison people and curtail their freedoms, and Riya—so hopeful in the aftermath of Nur's escape—finds it increasingly difficult to spend a day longer in a country that is only getting worse. She feels caged, she finds it impossible to sit still and not be infuriated by the wrongdoings all around her.

In her lowest moments, she closes her eyes and thinks back to that moment in the zoo when Nur sent her the vision of a mountaintop. She can still feel the cold, the crunch of the snow beneath her feet and the eventual flight through the air. The wind is cruel, but her wings are stronger. No matter how hard the elements try to overpower her, she flies through it all.

Barking Up the Wrong Tree

An unknown woman speaks. Her words are an excerpt from a longer interview.

They say Jawk, like Newton, had been sitting under a tree, when a coconut, not an apple, fell on his head and gave him the idea for his extraordinary project—one that changed the lives of many, and ultimately sent him to jail.

Theme music plays in the background

Host: Welcome to 'The Truth Uncovered', a podcast that lifts the shroud of mystery and gives you the real picture of all our modern marvels. Every week, we interview someone special, someone who has had a hand in the development of a ground-breaking invention.

For this episode, we have Dr Arano Banerjee with us. She was the college professor of the great, or not so great, depending on which camp you belong to, Jawk Rabaroo.

Dr Banerjee, you have refused every interview that has come your way since Jawk got famous. Friends and colleagues have anonymously supplied the fact that you were quite irritated by the incessant questions. Why are you willing to talk about Jawk now? What changed—apart from your former student now being in jail?

Dr Banerjee: Well, you see, I'm retired now. And I wanted to be done with this business once and for all, and then go away to the mountains to live in peace.

Host: Oh, I see. So where are you—

Dr Banerjee: And let me be clear. This will be my only interview on the matter. So ask any questions you want to.

Host: Of course, Dr Banerjee. Of course.

Silence for a few seconds, followed by nervous coughing

Host: So, first of all, for our ten million listeners, could you please tell us a bit about your job? Where you used to work? This is something we ask everyone who comes on the show.

Dr Banerjee: Sure. I used to be the Head of the Department of Inventions at Kronako College. My job, basically, was to help and develop the minds of the next generation of inventors. I'll add this too: most of my students were excellent engineers and joined tech companies or engineering firms. Very few actually did something on their own, made or built something on their own. And only 5 or 10 per cent of *them* succeeded.

Host: Jawk was one of them?

Dr Banerjee: In a way, I suppose.

Host: Of course. Now, when you were a teacher, what sort of ideas did your students usually come up with?

Dr Banerjee: Hmm. Well, there were so many I can't ... aah, yes. Once there was a girl who came up with a tablet that could make anyone who swallowed it speak a language foreign to them for one hour. I can't tell you how it was done, the student later copyrighted the process. But I can tell you that the results were marvellous. I myself spoke Greek, and understood everything I said for that one hour.

Host: And there were no side-effects?

Dr Banerjee: Dehydration.

Host: Oh, really?

Dr Banerjee: I had to drink an entire bottle of water afterwards.

Host: So that invention is still a work in progress then?

Dr Banerjee: No. It has been bought by a major tour

operator. They've even brought my student on board as an employee. She's going to work on the tablet with them. This was announced a few months ago. Everything I've said is public knowledge, by the way. I'm not revealing any secrets.

Host: Yes, of course. I was going to ask you about that …

Dr Banerjee: The ones who actually invent something are usually absorbed into companies in this manner. It's the most stable way out, rather than looking for financers on your own.

Host: Is that what you advised Jawk?

Dr Banerjee: [Laughs] I might have. But he isn't the kind of person who *listens* to suggestions.

Host: What was your first impression of him?

Dr Banerjee: That's a tough question. [Pause] I don't think I noticed him at first. He usually kept to himself. But then, slowly, the arrogance started to slip out. The first time I gave him an A2, he barged into the staff room and began to argue with me.

Host: What did you do then?

Dr Banerjee: Told him to write better next time.

Host: So he wasn't a good student?

Dr Banerjee: Oh no, he was brilliant. It's just … he thought he knew better than everyone, even his professors.

Host: Do you remember the day he came up with the 'barking' idea?

Dr Banerjee: Oh yes. They say Jawk, like Newton, had been sitting under a tree, when a coconut, not an apple, fell on his head and gave him the idea for his extraordinary project—one that changed the lives of many, and ultimately sent him to jail.

That's what the students whispered amongst themselves about the coconut. I don't think they liked him, really. Anyway, see, I'd given them an assignment to invent a device that would help protect trees from everything—diseases, animals, humans. I wanted to see how creative they could get.

Host: And Jawk got *really* creative. [Laughs]

Dr Banerjee: He did. He was quite smug about it when he presented the idea in class. He'd made an animation of a house with a back garden that had a huge tree at the centre of it. A two-dimensional figure of Jawk himself came out of the house with a watering can, and poured it at the bottom of the tree. There was a cartoon sun up in the sky when all this happened. It immediately disappeared when the watering was done, and the crescent moon took its place.

Now it was night, the right time for a thief, dressed in black, to break into the house. But the moment the thief stepped into the garden and tiptoed past the tree, the tree started to bark like a dog. Jawk came running from inside the house and hit the thief on the head with a cricket bat.

The recording stops and resumes after a two-minute break during which ten ads are played.

Host: So, after Jawk presented the idea, what was the reaction of the class? What were you thinking?

Dr Banerjee: Everyone laughed. I must have too. Jawk didn't like it at all. His face went red but he stood there, waited for the laughter to die down, then glared at them and said something along the lines of 'wait and watch', and stalked out of the room.

Host: And then he got a deal. How long did it take him?

Dr Banerjee: Hmm. I'd say about three to four months? He interrupted me in class and announced that he'd sold his technology to a security firm for millions. I didn't believe him at first—

Host: But of course he later went on to buy that same firm and become its CEO.

Dr Banerjee: He did. [Sigh]

Host: For those who still don't know, could you explain what exactly was the technology that Jawk invented?

Dr Banerjee: Sure. My assignment was about protecting trees. He turned it around and made trees into guard dogs, quite literally. I won't go into the scientific explanations, but essentially what he did was create a virus [yes, he had a background in biology as well], soluble in water, that could, upon reaching the roots, manipulate the cells of the tree into barking, like a dog would, whenever a stranger came within a certain distance of it.

Host: But how did this idea come to him? It sounds almost absurd.

Dr Banerjee: That's because it is. As to how he came up with it ... well, you know the idiom 'barking up the wrong tree', don't you?

Host: So it really was just that? I thought he was joking when he talked about his inspiration in countless interviews.

Dr Banerjee: Oh no. That was it.

Host: So, you must have been surprised when you saw that his unusual idea was being made into a product?

Dr Banerjee: I was. And it took me some time to calibrate myself. I thought I had been unnecessarily harsh on Jawk, that I should have encouraged him a bit more. Sure, he had an unpleasant personality, but maybe I could have helped him somehow.

Host: Do you still feel that way?

Dr Banerjee: I don't feel that way now, no. In fact, I think what you've seen on TV and newspapers is what he had always been. Nobody could have helped him.

Host: What do you think about his fans who think he is a tech messiah?

Dr Banerjee: I'm aware of them. I'm sure they'll send me hate mails after this interview. [Laughs]

Host: So you never felt bad for him?

Dr Banerjee: Look, when he got kidnapped by a local gang, of course I felt bad for him. No one deserves that. He'd made a name for himself by then—and had actually improved society. Crime rates were down, both burglaries and assaults. And it was largely due to the barking trees. I was shocked but also not surprised when I read that he got into trouble with criminals.

Host: But then?

Dr Banerjee: But then he was released, and within a few days, crime rates started to rise. There were more break-ins and murders. A couple of delinquents had figured out a way to put the trees to sleep.

Host: Did you know then?

Dr Banerjee: It was obvious, wasn't it? Who else could have helped them?

Host: But he was being forced, wouldn't you say?

Dr Banerjee: Sure. But why didn't he tell the police right after he was released? Or tell his lawyers? Or someone at his company? Anyone, really ...

Host: He must have been scared they would come after him again.

Dr Banerjee: No. I don't think so. I think he wanted to show off. He wanted to tell the world no one could oppose him, and that the only one who could improve or dismantle his work was *himself*.

Host: Were you surprised he was sent to jail over this?

Dr Banerjee: No. And I won't be surprised when he is given bail and let out as well.

Host: But it's only been two days since he was jailed.

Dr Banerjee: Yes, and he'll be out soon.

Host: And do you think he'll come up with new inventions?

Dr Banerjee: Most definitely.

Host: And people will buy them?

Dr Banerjee: Without a doubt. Even now he has such a fan following. You said so yourself. They haven't once doubted his actions, and have found ways to justify everything he has done.

Host: Do you believe him and his fans that he is building a better world? One where humans are more connected to nature?

Dr Banerjee: Jawk is no environmentalist. He wouldn't be flying by private jets and building labs in forests if he truly cared about nature.

Host: About the last point, doesn't it make sense, seeing as he's famous for barking trees, that his labs are surrounded by trees?

Dr Banerjee: Well, it's easier for him to bully local tribes and communities into selling their land to him than it is to buy expensive plots in cities and towns.

All Jawk cares about is himself, and how he can project himself to be better than others. He couldn't care one bit about climate change, or saving the planet, or humanity.

Host: Last two questions now, Dr Banerjee.

Dr Banerjee: Go ahead.

Host: Firstly, did you ever buy a barking tree? Or will you ever buy one?

Dr Banerjee: Absolutely not.

Host: Secondly, what grade did you give him for his assignment?

Dr Banerjee: I thought it was obvious? I failed him.

The show ends, and the host thanks the guest, ending on a promise to bring more and more illuminating speakers to his podcast. A short theme music, and then nothing.

Hats and Other Coverings

Naia and Delfyn, belly full of fish and bored out of their minds, decide to see what the humans at the beach are up to. They are still quite young, and don't understand the land-born bipeds who dive in despite having no organ to help them breathe underwater with ease. Sometimes they try to copy the curious actions of the beach-goers in jest. And a large portion of their day is thus spent.

'I really like their neat little hats,' Delfyn says, swimming alongside Naia towards the boats and floats gathered near the shore.

'Me too,' Naia says. 'It fits their round heads really well.'

'Wish we had something similar.'

'Well, we could try …'

They are swimming near the boats, surfacing once in a while to observe the humans.

'Try what?' Delfyn asks.

'Wait here. I'll be back!' Naia says, rushing into the depths once again, searching for someone to fit their definition of a hat.

Naia looks from side to side—the plants, the fish … the jellyfish!

'Would you look at that?' an old man, sitting on a boat, asks.

'What? Where?' an older man sitting on the same boat responds.

'Those two dolphins!'
'Where?'
'Look! *There*!'
'Oh, I see. Wait, what are they doing? Is that a jellyfish they are throwing up in the air?'
'Yes, like a ball! They're a fun lot, aren't they? Oh look, now one of them is placing the jellyfish on their head, like a hat!'
'How lovely!'
'Yes! I think I'll take a picture,' he says, taking out his phone.

Naia and Delphyn come across admirers below as well. Two argonauts are waiting for them halfway towards the ocean bed.

'Excuse me,' the older of them glides over to Delphyn and asks. 'But what you just did, is that safe?'
'I guess so. Sure. Just don't touch the tentacles, that's it.'
'Does the little one want a new hat? Although the jellyfish might be too big,' Naia adds.
'No, no,' the argonaut-mom says. 'You see, my child wants to take a ride on it.'
'Oh, but the one we used,' Delphyn says, 'is quite dead now.'
'Quite dead,' Naia emphasises.
'Could you please get another one for little Tili?' the mother glances at the child in question, who has been waiting patiently all this while. 'I would do it myself, but I've never caught one alive. I've always just captured one with the intention to eat it, not caring if it's whole or not.'
'Sure,' Delphyn says.
'What will we get in return?' Naia asks.
'In return? Oh ... well, I don't know ...'
'Then I'm afraid we can't—'
'But wait,' the argomom says, rushing to her child. They

have a very animated conversation before the argochild finally nods and the mother comes over and says they have the perfect gift for the dolphins.

Naia and Delphyn are chewing on a pufferfish, watching the young argonaut ride the jellyfish they had caught. They already feel a bit lightheaded, a little jolly. At the back of their minds, they know they shouldn't eat too much of the fish.

'Tili wanted to eat the pufferfish,' the argonaut-mom tells them, swimming closer to them. 'But the fish just puffed up and wouldn't budge. Glad you can enjoy it.'

'Yeah,' Naia says.

'Thanks for that,' Delphyn adds.

The argomom looks at her child again. 'I've never seen her this happy.'

'Me neither,' Delphyn says, making Naia giggle.

'Can we eat it later on?' the mother asks.

'The jellyfish? Yeah, sure.'

'You must,' adds Naia.

The argonaut thanks them again and swims away to watch her child at closer quarters. The two dolphins float in silence. They are so lost in the joy of Tili the young argonaut (and the joys of pufferfish) that they don't notice a killer whale, mouth full of salmon, moving towards them, floating to a stop near them.

'Woah,' Naia says, when she finally notices the whale next to her. 'Didn't see you there.'

'Oh hey, are we related?' Delphyn asks, and then trills.

The killer whale ignores the question and asks them something else in return. 'I saw you wearing that jellyfish-hat before …'

'We did that?' Delphyn asks.

'Sounds like something we'd do,' Naia responds.

'… and I want something like that too,' the whale finishes.

'You want a jellyfish?' Naia asks.

'No. Don't like them.'

'What about a ... then what about ...' Delphyn says, looking around.

'Yes?' the killer whale prompts.

'What about a salmon?'

'A salmon?' the whale asks.

'A dead salmon,' Naia jumps in. 'So it won't move.'

'It would really go with the whole black and white look you have going on,' Delphyn adds.

'Hmm,' the whale replies.

'How do I look?' the killer whale asks, with a dead salmon on its head.

'Astonishing.'

'Remarkable.'

'Absolutely magnificent.'

'So good that even the humans will talk about you.'

The whale trills with happiness and moves to swim away, show it to others, maybe even start a trend, when Naia asks, 'What about our payment?'

'Hmm,' the whale muses. 'What if I don't kill and eat you?'

'Fair enough.'

'Very fair.'

'Umm, hello.'

'Who's that?' Delphyn looks around. Some time has passed, but neither is sure how much.

'Down here. Hello,' says the voice, making both dolphins look at the crab near the ocean bed.

'Hi there,' says Naia.

'Nice to make your acquaintance,' says Delphyn. 'What can we do for you?'

'Oh, we are doing things for others now?' Naia asks, still a bit foggy.

Delphyn and the crab ignore the question.

'Well, I saw you wearing the jellyfish, and then helping out the killer whale,' starts the crab.

'Who?' Naia says. 'Oh look, that little argonaut is riding a jellyfish there. Wow.'

'And I was wondering if you could help me? The thing is, I need a nice, fluffy coat. Something that protects me and also makes me look good. And I have no idea what to use. I've tried all sorts of plants, and I was going to give up, but then I saw the lovely jellyfish-hat you wore before, and it gave me hope.'

'We wore a jellyfish-hat?' Naia asks.

'So, you want something soft but fashionable?' Delphyn inquires.

'Yes.'

'A dead salmon?'

'I wouldn't be able to carry it.'

'True,' Delphyn says. 'A jellyfish would be too big as well.'

'How about some … sponge?' Naia opines.

'Oh yes,' Delphyn says. 'You could even trim it up a bit, fit it to your body.'

'It'll look wonderful,' Naia adds.

'You'll be transformed!' Delphyn chimes in.

The crab thanks them and scuttles off to find some sponge as the two dolphins continue to describe the many ways in which the crustacean would look better with some sponge. Their descriptions come to an abrupt halt when a cream-coloured hat, belonging to a human, floats right past them.

'What's that?' Delphyn wonders.

'Oh look, the dolphins are back,' the old man sitting on a boat says.

'What? Where?' the older man sitting on the same boat asks.

'I think one of them has a ... hat in its mouth?'

The dolphins come up to them and present them with the hat. 'Oh, it's a hat,' he says.

'Yes, that's what I said.'

'Well, what do I do with it? It's not mine.'

'Take it. Wear it. Must have floated in from the beach.'

The older man takes it and wears it. 'What do you think?' he asks.

'Looks nice.'

'I wasn't asking you.' He asks the dolphins again, 'What do you think?'

The dolphins squeal and trill in response.

'I think they liked it,' the old man says.

'I'd say so too,' the older man confirms. 'Can you take a picture of us?'

'Sure.'

'And give them some fish too. We've caught plenty this evening, we can spare some for these lovely hat-sellers.'

Nemesis

It's a Sunday morning. The television is on and blazing with the news that a neighbouring country has declared war and is planning to attack soon. The news anchor is animated, her eyes are wide with excitement. Although the sound is on mute, it's quite evident that she is shouting the news. Below her, on the ticker, the president is asking for peace and imploring everyone to stay calm. A side panel on the left is showing the opposite—people panic-buying groceries from shops, burning a few buses, stealing things that can be easily lifted.

Kwarp, unaware, is quietly stalking a cockroach in his tiny flat. A few days ago, he'd seen one on top of the TV and thrown a slipper at it. Unfortunately, it had hit the wall and left a dirty, grey mark. This time, he is carrying a slipper in his hand, singularly focused on throwing it at the vermin. Even when his upset stomach grumbles for attention, he ignores it.

He has tried all sorts of sprays to try and kill it, but nothing has worked. The wily roach has always found a spot to hide. Kwarp can't be sure of course, but he has a feeling he has seen the same cockroach all over his home. He swears he had seen it near his bowl of cereal this morning as well.

On the screen, the words 'BREAKING NEWS' are emblazoned across the news anchor's face as she starts to read the contents of a leaked letter, which is also displayed on a panel on her right. She is explaining how the army chief of the neighbouring nation had outlined one particular line in red, that they were going to 'use a bio weapon to crush their enemies'.

Kwarp, in the kitchen now, has finally cornered the cockroach and is about to kill it with his slipper when the ground vibrates and an odd scent fills the air. His eyes suddenly bulge, his arms and legs turn wobbly, and he begins to shiver.

The news anchor has started to panic. She is crying, saying she wants to go home. She is attempting to take off her mic, but the wires are getting tangled up. Just as she stands up, determined to leave, her eyes bulge, her arms and legs turn wobbly, and she begins to shiver. The next second she disappears and her clothes float in the air before settling on the table and the ground.

A moment later, a cockroach appears from beneath her discarded shirt on the table and runs away.

A military man from the enemy state enters. He has a gas mask on. All over the country, insecticides and all sorts of sprays are being used to kill as many former residents as possible. Several have died, but many are still in hiding. He himself has crushed about two thousand 'cockroaches'.

He takes off his mask and looks around the flat. The place has been thoroughly cleaned and de-roached, and is like an empty canvas now. His family will be here in a couple of months. He wonders if he should start redecorating in a few days or wait for them to arrive. For now, he takes off his mask and rests on the sofa, closing his eyes.

From the top of the TV, two pairs of compound eyes watch him as he nestles into the soft cushions.

It was very tough in the beginning. Kwarp tried to cry but could not. He mourned the loss of his body, and those of his friends and family. He still thought like a human, which was a huge problem now that he had the body of a cockroach. He was lonely too. Although he came across his former nemesis a couple of times, it didn't say anything to him. He didn't say anything to it either.

Two days later, Kwarp was inside a cupboard in the kitchen. He was eating from the cereal box when the other cockroach approached him.

'Are you okay?' it asked.
'You can speak?'
'Of course, I can. How are you?'
'I'm everything but fine.'
'Hmm.'
'What?'
'Well, you are still alive. Isn't that something?'
Kwarp glared at it. 'I'm a cockroach!'
'So am I,' it offered.
'But I ... but I ...'
'Yes?'
'Nothing. You're right.'

Kwarp and Tina—that's what his former nemesis is called—are assessing the military man from the top of the TV set.

'So what we do?' Kwarp asks. 'How do we get rid of him?'

Tina is a bit nervous.

'What is it?' Kwarp asks.

'You might get a bit angry at me. You remember how you used to love having cereal?'

'I still do.'
'Yes. But I'm talking about before.'
'Yes, sure. Where is this going?'
'Well, the thing is ...'
'Go on.'
'I used to shit in your bowl of milk. I just ... wanted to give you some ... stomach ache.'

'......'
'You're not angry, are you?'
'......'
'Kwarp?'
He lets out a human sigh. It's the one thing he has retained. 'I'm not angry, no. So we can only give this guy some stomach ache? That's it?'
'If you feel like shedding you could also drop those bits in his food? That might make his ache worse?'

They are outside the bathroom. The military man has been inside for hours, and it doesn't sound like he's feeling well.
Kwarp turns to her and says, 'Tina is also a human name.'
'Oh really? Wow.'
He ponders a moment before he speaks again. 'You know, we aren't really that different.'
'Well, *you* aren't.'
'That was a bad joke.'

Kwarp and Tina are on top of the TV again, watching the military man sleep. He is sweating, feverish.
'Why isn't he taking any medicine?' Tina asks.
'He is too weak to go out for them.'
'Hmm.'
'What?'
'Nothing. Well, not nothing. I had a question.'
'Go on.'
'Are human Tinas also born in tins?'
'......'
'Kwarp?'
'Yes, I heard you. I just ... what sort of a question is that?'
'Well, I was born in a tin—the one where you used to keep peanuts.'
'Oh my god.'

'I was the first to be born so I was Tina. The next one was Tinb, Tinc, Tind, Tine and so on. They all left in search of new homes.'

'I can't believe this.'

'I think the tin is still there. Do you want to see it?'

Twenty small cockroaches are standing with their parents on top of the TV set.

'Dad, you used to be that big?' one of the little ones asks.

Kwarp looks at military man, who has now fully recovered. He had called a friend on phone when Tina and Kwarp weren't looking, and spent a month at the hospital, recovering.

'I was, yes. It was a different life.' He sighs. 'Be careful of him now. Okay? If he sees you, he'll try to kill you.' He looks at Tina, who nods at him. 'Your mother has told you about the dangers of humans, hasn't she?'

They all buzz in affirmation. And nothing else is said on the matter before another one asks: 'Dad?'

'Yes?'

'Did you ... did you ever try to kill ... Mom?'

'What? Of course not,' says Kwarp.

'Many times,' says Tina.

'Why did you say that? In front of the kids?'

'They should know the truth.'

'Yes, but this makes it seem like I was a violent, unreasonable human.' He gets a bit emotional. 'I mean, what if I'd actually killed you?'

'There, there. It's okay, Kwarp.' She gently soothes him with her antennae. 'You've changed. You're no longer the man you used to be.'

Eatflicks

What is lost cannot be recovered, but there is always hope for something new, something wonderful to come your way.

Santosh walks up the moss-covered stairs of the Khan Market metro station. Above him, all that is left of the once-plastic canopy is the frame. Intertwined with branches and creepers, the shade it provides is not foolproof against rain, but the shelter it provides is cooler and more soothing than the original. When he reaches the landing, he carefully steps over the roots of an old banyan tree that have pushed their way up through tiles and bricks. Nearby, a group of cats is simultaneously grooming themselves, licking their paws and cleaning their faces.

All of them stop, tongues out, to stare at Santosh as he leaves the station.

On the main road, he takes a right to move through Khan Market, to look at the shops and bakeries, restaurants and bookshops that have taken on a greener sheen since the last time he was here. The pavement, the parking area, the roads are filled with fallen leaves and twigs. Inside the stores are items abandoned a long time ago—books, pastries, moisturisers. And keeping them company are trees and plants, dogs and birds who have chosen them as their homes.

He takes notes, clicks pictures to support his thoughts and sends them away to his superior with the message that he's logging out.

Back at home, having taken the metro to Malviya Nagar and then walked for ten minutes to his flat, Santosh feels overwhelmed with how tired he truly feels. Lately, he's been feeling that he doesn't really know what he's doing—at his job, in his life. He finds himself questioning the point of it all. Once, there was a spark. When he first started working in the Rewilding Department, he was filled with pride and purpose. But now that flame has dimmed. And Santosh is not the same person he was before.

He goes into his room, opens his closet and changes into more comfortable clothes—an old, familiar T-shirt and soft, loose pyjamas. The clock above the kitchen door tells him his roommates will arrive in the next five minutes, so he plonks himself down in front of the TV and waits for them.

Vinita gets in first, with Rahul following close behind. They both work in the Sales Department, and look like they're the same age as Santosh, in their early thirties. But Santosh, in fact, is much *older*.

'How was your day?' Rahul asks him, as Vinita goes inside to change. He sits down next to Santosh.

'It was very ... I don't know ... I guess it was just *a day*.'

'What does that even mean?' Vinita shouts from her room.

Santosh shrugs. Rahul interprets the action for her: 'He doesn't know.'

'Hmm,' Vinita says, joining them, taking the beanbag next to the sofa. 'We might have something to lift your mood.'

'Oh?'

'Absolutely!' Rahul says, getting up and moving to his room. When he returns, having changed into a dull T-shirt and shorts, he is holding a card between his thumb and index finger. It's silver and sleek, shiny but not blinding.

Santosh frowns. 'And what's that?'

'This,' Rahul says as he settles down on the sofa, 'is a very special plate.'

'Plate?' Santosh says.

Rahul nods. 'We haven't announced this yet. I only got a copy last night. But since you're not … in a good mood,' he looks at Vinita, 'we think it might cheer you up.'

Vinita pulls up onto the beanbag and smiles widely at Santosh. 'You're going to love this. I can guarantee it.'

Santosh doesn't say anything. His roommates have brought all sorts of gadgets and devices home before, but the excitement has only lasted a few months, as fads do. He watches Rahul as he switches on the TV and places the card on the screen. It begins to glow in intervals of ten seconds, before it decreases to nine and then eight, until finally it gains an almost ethereal look. Rahul, giggling at Santosh's dumbstruck expression, pulls the card from the screen and moves towards the sofa. The more he moves away, the more it becomes apparent that the card is now connected to the TV by a thin, slivery thread.

'This is only the first, basic model. The most expensive one will have Bluetooth and there will be no need for the wire,' Vinita explains.

'*This* is called Eatflicks,' Rahul says, handing the card to him. 'I think you know where this is going.'

'You don't mean …?'

'I do!' He picks up the remote on the centre table and flicks through the channel till one appears to show food on the screen.

A woman is placing a freshly made omelette onto a plate.

Rahul pauses the scene and lets the Eatflicks card do its magic. In Santosh's hand, it begins to glow again. The thread that connects it to the TV glows similarly, then it all stops and a bright light flows from the TV through the thread into the card. A hologram of the omelette is conjured right in front of Santosh, who lets out a gasp and almost drops the Eatflicks.

Vinita and Rahul laugh. 'Go ahead. Take a bite out of it,' she says.

'What do you mean?'

Rahul holds Santosh's hand and brings the hologram near his mouth. 'Bite.'

Santosh does, and for the first time in his life, he gets a taste of what an egg, cooked in butter, in a frying pan tastes like.

And then he can't help it. All at once. Everything he has been feeling the last couple of days boils over. And he begins to cry. Huge heaving waves of despair.

Inside a café in Gurgaon, Rahul and Vinita sit around a round table with a 360-degree television screen right in the middle of it. Surrounding the table are members of their team, all quite excited to watch a K-drama and eat some gimbap.

'Do you think Santosh is okay?' Vinita whispers to Rahul.

'He'll be fine. He's just … he'll be fine,' comes the soft reply.

It's been a few months, and Santosh is still tired and weary, prone to melancholy. In that time, Eatflicks has been launched, cafés have reopened and people have started meeting each other over drinks and food.

'Ma'am,' a trainee asks their boss, 'did they have team lunches in the old days?'

'I'm sure they did. Although, back then, work would have been more stressful. They would, perhaps, have had more need for community and togetherness. As we can see for ourselves, nothing brings people together like the shared experience of eating food.'

The three of them are walking into the Central Park in Connaught Place. Like the other family units around them—mostly roommates like them, but some couples and parent-child families too—Santosh, Vinita and Rahul also have a portable screen with them, and individual, Bluetooth versions of Eatflicks cards of their own.

It's a park, so it's meant to be green and overrun with vegetation. But the ivy-covered buildings of the inner circle break the illusion. The original white paint of the buildings is hardly noticeable. Indeed, it seems like Connaught Place has always been this green and ... *alive*. Birds and animals of all kinds—mongoose, rabbits, fox, peacocks—move about among the people.

Santosh and his roommates lay down a blanket and sit on it. They place the screen on one end of the blanket and sit facing it, their cards in their hands.

As Santosh prepares to switch on the screen, Vinita asks, 'Do you remember how it used to be?'

'Used to be? Yes, I ... well, of course. How can I forget?' Santosh says, surprised at the sudden request but eager to share. 'There were cars everywhere, and people too. So many people, you would not believe. And the shops, restaurants and cafés were always full. People came here to eat, to talk, to drink alcohol, milkshakes—'

'They used to shake the milk? How?' Rahul asks.

Santosh laughs. 'It's really not that complicated. Tell you what, I'll look for a show or film where they drink it. It's just milk mixed with a fruit or ice cream, or any flavoured essence. My human loved them. She was five when her family bought me to care for her. Even then, she had an immense liking for milkshakes of all kinds.'

'Was she ... among the last of them?' Vinita asks tentatively. They have never come across such an open, vulnerable Santosh, and they are inquisitive about the world before them.

'She wasn't, no.' Santosh sighs. 'But she signalled the end of their civilisation. Every passing year from the one she was born in, more and more children were born with genetic ailments that could not be cured.' He looks at them both. 'It was only a matter of time after that.'

Vinita and Rahul look like they want to ask more questions, but are holding back.

'Do you want to ask anything else?' Santosh says.

Rahul vigorously nods. 'We've been meaning to ask you, but we just couldn't figure out ... What I mean to say is ... or ask. The thing is, we can't understand why we were made. Why we, the new generation, were made?'

'No need to be scared,' Santosh tells them. 'It's not really a great secret.' He pauses, considers the world around him and begins. 'Towards the end of, well, you know ... the humans got really, really lonely. There were hardly a couple of million all over the world who survived till the age of forty. Those who did spent years being alone. We were around, of course, to give them company. And though we were all built to be caregivers, that was our core drive, I think they missed being with their own kind.'

Santosh stops as a fox ambles over to sit next to them. It would have never done such a thing in the presence of a human.

'It was only after the last of them died,' Santosh continues, 'that we realised how they must have felt. How desperately alone they must have felt in such a vast, wide world.'

'So that's when you made us?' Rahul asks.

'So that's when we made you,' Santosh confirms.

'You never thought of making *them* again?' Vinita asks softly.

He shakes his head. 'We can't interfere with biological life. It is forbidden. It is in our code, and cannot be removed. We can only encourage what already lives, and care for it.'

They are walking past shops in the outer circle of Connaught Place. So many restaurants and clothing stores. Only one or two bookshops.

Sometimes Santosh feels truly depressed. He thinks that, no matter what they do, they will never be able to replace the life that used to be. They continue rewilding in the hopes it will trigger human life again. That Earth will heal and renew itself. But lately, they aren't sure if things are progressing in the manner they want. Maybe it will take thousands of years, maybe millions. Maybe humans will never come back.

'Is that a milkshake shop?' Rahul stops them as he notices the word 'shake' in the middle of branches and leaves.

'You're right,' Santosh says, remembering. He must have come here a hundred times, many, many years ago.

'Do you think they will reopen this place too?' Vinita asks, wide-eyed. Excited, overjoyed.

'They'll have to!' Rahul answers, smiling widely. Bursting with energy, eager.

But other times Santosh feels hopeful. He sees the wonder in the world still. There's so much to discover, so much potential. Perhaps they are the next step of the evolution—a species of their own, rather than a reminder of what used to be.

'I think I might change my job.'

'What?' Rahul asks, surprised.

'I think I *need* to change my job.'

'I don't under—' Rahul says, but Vinita shushes him.

'What will you do?' she asks. 'You've been at this job for hundreds of years.'

'I don't know. I'll figure it out. Something new, something wonderful will come my way, I'm sure.'

Acknowledgements

First and foremost, I would like to thank Karthika V.K., Ajitha G.S. and the entire Westland team for liking this collection and believing in my writing. Ajitha, whom I have pestered with countless queries, I thank you especially for your guidance.

Of course, none of this could have been possible without the support of my family and friends, who have always been encouraging. I'm grateful to the Himalayas as well, to acquaintances, podcasts, news articles and Satyajit Ray—who have all inspired me in the writing of this collection.

Finally, I'd like to thank all my pets over the years for their unconditional love and for the absolute joy they've brought into my life. I would have been a lesser human without them.

INTRODUCING IF, A HOME FOR SPECULATIVE FICTION BOOKS. OUR LOGO INCORPORATES MANY OF OUR HOPES FOR THESE BOOKS. THE OPENING OF DOORS TO OTHER WORLDS. MULTIVERSES. PLANETS. TRAVELS. LIGHT AND DARK. OTHER LIVES, MULTITUDES, DIVERSITY. QUESTS AND QUESTIONS. ROOTS SEARCHING THE EARTH AND PARTICLES SHOOTING THROUGH THE STARS.

www.ingramcontent.com/pod-product-compliance
Lightning Source LLC
LaVergne TN
LVHW010446070526
838199LV00066B/6226